The Story of
the Stone

The Story of
the Stone

Tales, Entreaties & Incantations

James Kelman

ISBN: 979-8-88744-106-1 (paperback)
ISBN: 979-8-88744-107-8 (hardcover)
ISBN: 979-8-88744-116-0 (ebook)
Library of Congress Control Number: 2024943055

Cover by Drohan DiSanto
Interior design by briandesign

10 9 8 7 6 5 4 3 2 1

PM Press
PO Box 23912
Oakland, CA 94623
www.pmpress.org

Printed in the USA.

for Philip and Roslyn

Contents

Acknowledgments

James Kelman thanks Other Press, Canongate Books, thi wurd and Tangerine Press for permitting the inclusion of stories from their publications.

Introduction

I was always a reader. If a book came recommended by a friend I tried to read it. Sometimes I failed. The writing was hopeless. The guy who loaned me the book might agree about the boring bits but would ask about the story, what about the story, did you like the story?

That was a hard one, did I like the story, separating the story from the writing of the story. Ignore the writing, enjoy the story. Skip the boring bits, go with the "story itself." I found this level of awareness difficult to accept as a young writer. What is the "story itself." Is it "the action." But what is action in a book? Reading is one of the least physical pastimes I know. What makes action? Is it turning the page? When we read a book about a war it involves the same activity as reading one about collecting buttercups. The reason I got a book was to read it. I didn't want a book not to read. Even if it was yet another Explosive!! Million Dollar!! Bestseller!! from Robert Simpson, whose tales of all-action super-heroes are purchased by the ton by the cultural wing of NATO Ltd., dished out gratis to troops and boy-soldiers everywhere.

Imagine the visual artist: ignore how I paint this scene, just enjoy the view. Ignore how I've painted the old lady, just picture her for yourself. Ignore how I've sculpted the figure, says the sculptor, just see the person.

Artists are makers. A writer is a maker. A writer of fiction makes a story. A story about an old man is a story about an old man, not the creation of a human being of advanced years. I outgrew writers who didn't work on the basics. That was the job. Do the basics and you find a story. It's your story. The teller of the story tells the story. The storyteller should not throw a pile of words at the reader and tell them to find it themselves.

I loved stories as a boy. I enjoyed hearing them and I enjoyed telling them. That is what we do as human beings. Each of my grandmothers told stories, maternal and paternal. My maternal grandmother heard Gàidhlig from her grandparents. My paternal grandmother heard it every moment of every day. It was how she thought. She belonged to the culture. She lived and breathed the language, the tradition.

In ordinary working life people are forever telling stories. Factory workers, people in working-class jobs, they don't have time to call their own. Listen to these old-timers who tell a tale with a straight face right to the bitter end. This kind of story can be told in a factory anywhere in the world, rather like jokes in the school playground. Tell them fast and write them fast. We're used to it in song, but there's space in literature too. "Phantom 309" is a story—no it's not, it's a song.

In the 1970s people referred to my short tales as "prose poetry" and presumed they were paying me a compliment. Poetry is sublime. Prose is prosaic. Cheeky bastards. The superiority of poetry to prose was a class issue. I wanted to punch them on the mouth. I knew that the veriest most brief of stories was always a story, if this is what it was, and not a poem, unless that is what it was. By then I had discovered non-English-language cultures. I sought freedom and all of those discoveries helped me find that freedom. So much so that I took it for granted, such that I found the greatest of all freedoms: to not give a fuck.

I composed a story in the form of a woman and called it an Abstract Story, hoping to upset the critics who thought Concrete Poetry the absolute bee's knees and shuddered at the idea of factory life, tales of factory life—anything derived from the shopfloor, or the backstreets and alleys trod by the distorted shadows of the faceless multitudes.

Different fonts for different stories. Why not? That was an interesting line to follow, and one I explored eagerly. I had begun working life at the age of fifteen, in a printing factory. People told stories all the time. I listened, agog. Everything was just so fucking incredible, just fucking unbelievable! I went home and told my pals about one auld guy in particular. He used variations of the word *fuck* in umpteen ways, and never once in reference to the sexual act. In my community the word *fuck* was never used in that context. His yarns made yer toes curl. My pals appreciated them too, the way the auld guy telt them.

Nay wonder man they were fucking brilliant and I wantit to fucking do it exactly like it was, like he done it man just fucking telling it, didnay fucking matter how it soundit what-ever it was man fuck ye never fucking knew like know what I mean how they came fucking oot man, fucking laugh, just fucking man whatever it was the story some stupit cunt man usually himself, he ended up man whatever just like story eftir story the way he telt them man ye just fucking know what I'm saying, bastards, getting the fucker, just like how he telt it, the fucking story man the way he telt it, trickier than it fucking looks and I wantit to get them, spot on cause if ye didnay there wasnay a fucking story. Nay story man, no if it wasnay him telling it. Ye needed to hear him, so that was what I tried with my pals, telling them, the way he telt them, they were just so fucking wonderful man I just found it like fuck sake, how his missis ever put up with the cunt I dont fucking know man fucking divorces and aw that jesus christ man ha fucking ha fucking ha ha man know what I'm saying, the fucking missis she woulda fucking clobbirt him man, she woulda stuck a knife in the auld cunt's belly, if ever she fun oot, auld Jeannie man that was her name, if ever she fun oot, he telt me, he telt me that himself and I'm no kidding.

I didn't resist telling the old guy's stories to my family members. Such a thing did not enter the reckoning. It was not possible. Without the old guy telling the story there was no story. No matter how good I was in recounting the story after the fashion of the old man, no. I couldn't tell them to anybody except my pals. Him telling the stories was unacceptable. There was no separation. The stories didn't exist, neither did he, except within the factory. When it came 5 o'clock and the factory hooter sounded, he was among the first out the door, a slight figure. I think he had grandkids. Did he tell them his stories? Doubtful.

I was an apprentice compositor. The apprentice learns by taking apart what the journeyman compositor has composed. Apprentices study the page as they learn to compose. They judge space. When a line isn't centred correctly a compositor sees this without having to measure. They learn to spot typographical and other spacial inconsistencies before it gets to the printer, and if they don't then that page will have to be taken apart and re-set properly.

Gill Sans and Times Roman were the most common fonts in ordinary jobbing work. Those were in constant production, and the type used on each job was scrapped afterwards. Apart from those most other fonts were used whenever necessary, until the typeface on individual pieces of lead type had lost its facial features.

Once a page had been printed, the apprentice distributed each piece of lead type back into the font case. The font case was a particular style of cupboard designed to that purpose. Each size of each font had its own drawer within the cupboard. Each style of each font had its own drawer, bold or italics, within the font cupboard.

I discovered there was no such thing as "space." Every so-called "space" was a piece of lead, or aluminium, or wood, or plastic. But what is a "piece"? Take it apart, take the part apart.

In those days a compositor composed the page and was responsible for every aspect of that, including the space between letters, between words, between lines of words. Is it "space" or "spaces"? In ordinary typesetting work each letter and letter-space was its own tiny piece of lead type. "Spaced" was an instruction to the compositor. It meant that tiny slivers of lead were to be inserted between each letter. After the job was done, every sliver of lead had to be distributed back into its rightful compartment. A boy's nimble fingers made the job less troublesome. Journeymen's fingers were thicker and found the work more difficult

I liked exploring the old font cases, and seeing some of the ancient typefaces. There were rows of storage units and I crawled around the floors checking out the lower drawers, fumbling around and within the cobwebs. Some were never used and hadn't been for years. But they were kept. Of course they were kept.

The typesetting and visual layout of the page was crucial. Whether or not a paragraph should be indented depends on the story. At one time I needed the paragraphs of first-person stories separated by one line spacing and rendered without indentation. I didn't want it, I needed it; the story required it. The "I-voice" character didn't exist otherwise.

In short stories particularly I needed the freedom to do whatever I wanted. And what I wanted was the story, whatever that story was, what it is, that is what I wanted, and to set it out there, just as it is.

You have to fight for your own spelling and punctuation, on behalf of your characters who cannot exist without it. In one story I had to spell "definitely" as "definately," for some but not all uses. My editor hated it: Oh God Jim they will just think we cannot spell.

Okay but that's our problem, not the character in my story. Either he exists or not.

At least be consistent!

I can be consistent. So too my characters but their consistency is not mine. They have their own existence. If my character cannot spell "correctly" then I am not going to correct it. My characters are always consistent, unless I've failed them.

Publishers have their own "house style." They want to impose uniformity on you. If you write a pile of short stories each one might feature a different first-person narrator and the language may vary from story to story, as between different individuals. Everybody uses language in their own way. So I didn't want that house style imposed. How could my characters breathe? They would suffocate. How would I breathe! I hate that sort of imposition; standard English literary form, fuck them and their hegemony, imperialist bastards. Let the individual breathe. If they cannot breathe they do not live. How can your characters tell their own stories in somebody else's language?

I was berated by an editor who eventually lost her temper altogether. A character of mine kept using the word *cunt*. My editor said to me, "Why don't you insult the male member some of the time?" What do you mean "you"? It isn't me, I'm not the one saying "cunt," it is the character. If it was up to me I would get him to say "prick" but "prick" is not part of his vocabulary, not in that context. When he uses the word *prick* he either refers to somebody who acts foolishly, or refers to the penis. When he uses the word *cunt* he never refers to the vagina.

I began doing away not only with quotation marks to distinguish dialogue but any means at all of distinguishing dialogue from narrative. Some writers used a dash but I thought the dash was clumsy, aside from the fact that it performs the same function as quotation marks. Some writers used nothing at all. I was with them. But greater precision was essential. Was a character speaking, or thinking? I wanted that ambiguity. I was looking to abandon any separating device as between dialogue and narrative, between the inner and outer worlds: a route that allowed entry into the inner psyches, the subjective perspective, into the mind of the characters. Only in that way could I create stories from within their own world. I did not want the characters' world distinguished from that of the narrator.

Also, once you separate the inner world from the outer world you land in old philosophical quandaries. There are political consequences too; issues around the struggle for self-determination, linguistic hegemony, and so forth. There is not the space to go into it here. Style has nothing to do with it. Style is an intrusion. To discuss a writer's style is to insult their craft.

A musician composes on a guitar one day but maybe on keyboards the next, or switches to a different instrument to see if it helps move the thing on. One of my favourite songs as a fourteen-year-old was Del Shannon's "Runaway." How would it have been without the keyboards? A musician friend of mine, George Gallacher, once did an arrangement of this and the only way he could get it in any way satisfactory was to replace the keyboard by whistling. It's a beautiful arrangement. It completely changed the song to a reflective piece for fifty-year-olds.

Artists not only create individual visual perspectives, the means they use are individual. They apply paint in different ways, mix the paint in different ways. It depends on the work, the composition. Everything, anything; going wherever, utilising freedom. I envied Cézanne, Rodin and Modigliani. I wanted everything in there. Self-referential artworks. I didn't want anything from the outside. The short prose of Franz Kafka, Jorge Luis Borges's *Book of Imaginary Beings,* two collections by Gertrude Stein: volumes I and II of *The Previously Uncollected Writings*: *Reflection on the Atomic Bomb* (1973) and *How Writing Is Written* (1974). Other literary cultures have their place. Things don't stand alone:

everything is something, and the compositor or the artist is responsible for everything, not just the words but the spaces between, just as writers and artists take from anywhere and everywhere, and demand that right. Action is back to front and inside out. A blank canvas isn't nothing. There is no nothing. Japanese writers were influenced by the stories of Edgar Allan Poe. Poe returns me to my own intellectual tradition here in Scotland: the primacy of the individual, the uniqueness of the perception, and the three-way expression of that, which is the exploration of time and space.

My paternal grandmother was from the Outer Hebrides. The Ceilidh was fundamental to her culture. People sang and gossiped, told tall tales, sad stories and meandering ballads with plenty pauses. Some they put to music, and sometimes played the music with no words at all. That was her tradition, which is our tradition, except that we made fun of it, made fun of her, made fun of ourselves. The laugh was on us. Not one of us learned the language, the language of our grand-mother, the language of our family. We were taught not to notice and were content in that. We were never given the opportunity and we did not grab it for ourselves. It's on our own head. The imperialist taught us not to value our family.

When I was a boy and the family were gathered round the television she sat near the screen, but swivelled round to watch us. She watched us watching the screen. We found it comical and a bit embarrassing. She laughed and made derogatory comments, stabbed the nearest body with her walking stick; she clapped her hands and got that beat:

> Hoh roh hurreee oh hoh hoh
>
> Hoh roh hurreee hurreee
>
> Hoh roh hurreee oh hoh hoh
>
> Hoh row hee roh hoh hoh hoh

The Story of the Stone

I pass this stone around the room. Make sure that everyone here holds the stone. No one must pass it along as though beyond reach.

Yes, in your left hand. Hold it as I do, as I here exhibit. Yes, and now inside your left hand, in the valley of the palm. How the stone here is as it were locked in, do you feel it?

And your right hand like this, exhibiting the movement, the bludgeoning action abrupt or not, as to work, work, see how you work!

When it arrives back at myself I shall continue the story of the stone.

Meantime I say to you that the stone is of our species. See! This stone has been nurtured.

fruits of Empire

Graduate students are advised that the proper context for such a debate might begin from the late 1950s, and the work of the outside broadcasting units that occurred during the making of the Early Fruits of Empire series. The particular location cannot be ascertained. The team broadcast live from a streetmarket on the outskirts of a city thought to be in the central Sub-Continent or Middle Eastern regions; earlier rumours suggested southern Africa. There is a dearth of accredited information. In those days there was neither email nor social media. We know that the television production team requested that the male presenters dress in "tribal garb," as the memo-exchange described it: loin cloths, kilts, shields, hoops and bangles. There was no disrespect intended.

The film-crew operated from a jam-packed urban roadway using dual cameras. Limited back-up was available. The production team had hoped to hire local workers. Nothing further is known on that. Certainly locals in their tens of thousands would have thronged the market roadways and side-alleys, as they had done since time immemorial. Animals of every domestic species were employed, bought and sold, and others too might have been procured at a price. Goats and oxen pulled carts, while on either side of the thoroughfares were stalls, barrows and makeshift stores defined by blankets spread on the ground. An entire area was given over to the marketing of old bicycles and their parts. Another specialized in tools of every description; interior sections dealt with plumbing, carpentry and electrical wares. Close by was mechanical farming equipment, alongside boring and cutting tools, rust-coated machinery from earlier centuries. Along the wynds, lanes and darker off-road locations one found the weaponry, armoury and defence implements. Those were acquired from foreign powers and for use in neighbouring provinces. Solitary individuals prowled and gestured at passersby, displaying unknown produce and articles from within the folds of their body coverings. In any space unoccupied by sellers and their helpers were beggars in diverse forms and shape, and of each and every deficiency known to the species. Here everything that might be sold was for sale.

On the third day was the first day of the shoot. During lunchbreak the crew members strolled in and around the market. One acquired a strangely shaped walking-cane from a ground-store. There were two researchers attached to the team. They were intrigued by the find. They discussed it with the executive producer and the female and male presenters of the programme. The consensus was that this was not a walking-cane. More likely it was a war-club, estimated three hundred and fifty years old, gnarled but relatively unwarped. A detailed description and photocopy of the cane/club were faxed to experts in the field. Later that morning they received the reply. Its provenance was vouchsafed but its place of origin could not be identified. It was thought not to be local, but that its provenance might relate to several pre-cultural hoards not yet quantified within the Crown property ruling.

Experts agreed that its value to specialist-collectors might be taken for granted. The mystery of its origin gave it an additional aura, which bestowed upon it enigma-status. Both researchers to the programme confirmed that the sale of this single relic might secure the future of two entire villages for a period of ten years, perhaps longer. They and the couple presenting the programme crossed the roadway, followed by the two-man sound and camera crew, seeking to find the rear area ground-stall where the transaction took place and record the meeting with the original seller. They hoped to acquire more detailed information on the artefact, and advise the owners of the good news in regard to external value. There were no further developments. This was the last stage of the shoot. None of the recorded minutes was ever recovered. There were rumours and these may be followed up with requisite permissions. Neither presenter returned to the series. The news embargo is now lifted. None of the broadcasting unit remains with us. Graduate students with an interest in our earlier outside broadcasting services should apply to the department.

Identifying the nonexistent

Genocide too, you will find a way to identify people without naming them. What you do here is create an exception. If I am in control I give this exception a category. Here now is this category of exceptions. Everybody exists except people who fall into this exceptional category. We have not named them. We point to their attributes, characteristics, markers and features. Allow the algorithm, it too has a use-value. We shall identify them. They are the people. See, we identify them. They are the one and only ones. But as to whether they truly are the "nonexistent," no, that is outwith my remit, what we refer to as "remit." They are to be identified and we identify them. Seek the one who is remitted, who is to follow me, we are linked irrevocably, as the inference relates, and reveals.

The Sensitivity of the Artiste

I dont know what happened. We were there for the performance which was outstanding. We knew it would be. He was outstanding and he always was outstanding. Surely he knew that? Surely he knew our estimation of his work? One would have expected as much. Although who knows, perhaps for the likes of us who had borne witness to past occasions, the various visits he had made during the full many years, the evaluation, the evaluation we endeavour to place, perhaps all of that, whatever it amounts to and who knows, is too much or perhaps insufficient from we critics and friends, and an artist such as himself will be left uncertain, withdrawn and might we say, "secretive."

There is no "one" value we can place on such. People will come to him in their own individual ways. In my estimation he was always wonderful. On some occasions more wonderful than others, it is not too much to say. This matter he addressed at the Q A session where his first answer was the more impressive. It was not an "answer" but a statement, he halted the questioner in order to deliver it. The Chairperson should have waited until people were back in their seats.

This was why so few heard or had given it their full attention. Many failed to realise he had delivered the statement. Obviously a few people heard. Perhaps they could have acknowledged this. It was unfortunate and not even ironic. Certainly I would never have blamed them. If this is what he did, and he does seem to have blamed them. Perhaps that is significant. People were acting after that fashion. How did they know, they were only returning to their seats. People were still full of the performance. It had only just finished. Really and truly, people were moved. They were in the flush of that, enthusing to one another. There are plenty reasons why his statement, whatever it was—declaration—would have gone unheard.

I would never lay blame too easily, too readily. We assume the outstanding ones are as they are in every direction.

Or was he just overly sensitive. People are, and for one reason or another; perhaps several. There were some in the audience felt sorry for him. I was not one of those. Not at all. There was no reason for such. We passed within his hearing on our way to the exit. You were outstanding, I said, dont worry.

He looked at me.

I glanced back before we reached the exit, he was gazing off somewhere, alone in himself.

Life & Death Matters

Theresa thought I would die but she was wrong. There was no chance of that, not presently. I would die before her but, and this she held against me, that would be later. For now, I was improving.

Days later. I had recovered. She was scolding me over some triviality. It moved into the life and death issue yet again. Oh god. My sigh was too loud and she glared at me. This was a serious matter. More serious for who? It's me recovering from illness, I said.

She sighed. I know that.

So it is your fault that here we are arguing.

We're not arguing and it's not my fault if we are.

I shrugged. She was waiting for me to say whatever I was going to say. I stayed silent.

I know you want to argue the case, she said, dont hold back for me.

I dont want to argue the case. It's only how sometimes I feel like I've got to ignore the present in order to answer your comments. This stuff about dying, really, I cannot be bothered with it. It gets me down having to discuss it so often, especially when I'm either on my sick bed or struggling to get out the damn thing.

Theresa smiled, shaking her head. You would never die before me, she said.

Here we go again, I said, yes, it would be so so unfair if I did! And I smiled, hoping she too would smile. The irony would maybe work to hold us together.

But she didnt notice. If she did it had no impression. She knew where she headed and would get there with or without my assistance.

Sorry, she said, and I shut my eyes. It was always bad when she apologized. The worst was yet to happen. I looked for the aspirin. She had entered that absent-minded mode, located someplace at the depth of her own world. It was no minor psychological attribute, rather a sweeping all-embracing thing that prepared me for a faux pas committed twenty years ago. Even though I would happily die, she said, honestly, if I knew or even believed you might live forever.

I fainted, metaphorically. Then stopped smiling because what she said had me flummoxed in a way that almost induced laughter. Pardon? I said. That's not even a sentence.

She didnt answer, thank heaven. I thought about what she said but she had made so fine a point I could not understand what it was and the more I tried the less I knew. I tried to recall the words and the order of utterance, as a way of putting it, but it had gone altogether. I smiled but she pounced on this. No, I said, shrugging. I just eh ... could you repeat what ye said?

She stared at me.

Honestly, I said.

Dont say honestly when you arent being honest.

Pardon? It was you that said "honestly."

Oh I cannot bear this.

Well dont blame me for that if it was you.

Even to consider such a thing. I didnt think you ever would do that. This is so very far down the line. I didnt realize we had reached this stage.

What? What stage?

Oh God. I dont know where I stand.

Well that is hardly my fault, twenty years later, whatever it is you mean, I dont know what you mean. I dont even remember what you said, I cannot recall the actual words, just the word, and the order.

I cannot even talk to you any longer, it is so horrible.

Well I cant talk to you either.

You said something and it's horrible.

Pardon. Here we are fighting. How come we're fighting!

I'm not fighting.

Oh for heaven sake.

I'm not.

I'm just not capable of it, incapable of it. It's me that's ill.

I thought you had recovered.

I have recovered.

Well why are you saying you're ill?

I'm not ill.

You're saying you are. You promised!

I'm not ill.

Oh God, you promised me.

I'm not ill. Sorry, I'm sorry, I should never have said it.

You promised.

Yes but I cant control it, if I am, if I'm not. Anyway, I'm not ill at all.

I cant bear it if you are.

I'm not.

She sighed.

Really, I said and stepped to her and put my arms round her, down by the small of her back and kissed her forehead. I smiled. I would never ever, I said.

She nodded.

Some things are too difficult.

I could not worry unduly about it. The doctor had given no grounds to believe something evil would befall, not without warning, although who believes doctors these days. It is not their fault, but why cover up the deficiencies of an inhumane system. I had been prepared for something awkward or even worse, I failed to mention it to him. It is not precise to say "failed." I had nay intention of so advising him a very long strand of tissue had issued from my throat on three separate occasions. I assumed it was intestinal. One hears horror tales, certain types of worm or tapeworm. That he had found five insects inside my belly was unexpected in the extreme but perhaps less than 100%. Within our wider family the eating habits of myself and male siblings are greeted by giggles and guffaws. Yes we "eat anything," but only virtually. Nothing inedible, not by intention anyway. There are reasons for that which are irrelevant to this, reasons also for the insects but these too are irrelevant, and I should leave it at that.

A History

When from out of the evening the quiet reached such a pitch I had to unlock the door and wander abroad. At this time the waves ceased pounding the rocks and the wind entered its period of abeyance. Along the shore I travelled very casually indeed, examining this, that and the other, frequently stooping to raise a boulder. That absurd and unrealized dream from childhood, that beneath certain boulders ...

I was going south to south-east, towards the third promontory. It was where I could take my ease at times such as this. A fine huddle of rocks and stone. There were three little caverns and one larger one, a cave; this cave would presently be dry. It always afforded a good shelter. From it I could gaze out on the sea. I withdrew my articles from my coat pocket, a collection of shells. Even now I retained the habit, as though some among them would prove of value eventually. I leaned close to the entrance of the cave and chipped them out in a handful, not hearing any splash due to the roaring of the waves. Yet there too had been a striped crab shell of a sort I was unfamiliar with, about five inches in diameter. I kept an assortment of items at home to which this crab shell might have proved a fair addition. In all probability, however, the stripes had simply been a result of the sea's turmoil. Or perhaps it had been wedged in between two rocks for several centuries. I doubted my motives for having thrown it away. But I had no history to consider. None whatsoever. I had that small collection of things and too the cottage itself, its furnishings and fittings, certain obvious domestic objects. But be that as it may not one of these goods was a history of mine. My own history was not in that cottage. If it could be trapped anywhere it would not be there. I felt that the existence of a dead body would alter things. Previous to this I had come upon a dead body so I did have some knowledge. It had been a poor thing, a drowned man of middle age, a seaman or fisherman. I made the trip to the village to convey the information then returned to the cottage to await their arrival. I had carried the body into there and placed it on the floor to safeguard against its being carried back out on the tide. The face was bearded, no boots on the feet though a sock remained on the left foot. A man in the sea with his wits about him, ridding himself of the boots to assist the possibility of survival. He would have had a family and everyday responsibilities whether to them or to his shipmates; that amazing urge to survive which is itself doomed. He would have been dead in twenty minutes, maybe less. If I had been God I would have allowed him to survive for twenty hours.

But now here I was. And could it be described as good, this lack of damp, not being chilled to the bone; even a sensation of warmth. All in all I was wishing I had kept a hold of the shells and that striped one of a crab, and I would then have been very content indeed, simply to remain there in the cave, knowing I would only have to travel such and such a distance back to the cottage.

It was always her

On the Sunday before it happened she was there by the window. She was central to it. That is how it was. Ours is a good-sized curved window, style Glasgow, with its alcove, so nothing special. The snow had fallen heavily for most of the morning and early afternoon and way way over down the Sandbank Street hill young folk were sledging and enjoying that snow, real snow, real deep and great and they were not used to it and prone to taking chances, young people gambling, life and limb; these thoughts dont enter their brain—never, and not just young people, that is how we are.

Snowman weather. They dont see much of that in this place. A couple of days per winter they bring out the sledges. Not much more. I'm saying this is how it was.

And her favourite radio station playing. So this was the Sunday, and the last quarter of an hour of the show. We listened to it most weeks. She it was. I wouldnt have bothered. She had her likes, she always did. This was good music, roots music, and the organist playing, a blues musician, that nice jazz-funk, reminiscent of Jimmy Smith and she was standing gazing out, arms folded, swaying sideways to the music, the woollen bootees, and the jogging trousers, the chunky cardigans, all relaxed here in her own home, while outside was beyond, beyond. These elements, as if they were hers, hers alone but that was what she had forgotten, that she wasnt alone, rocking back and forth, she had forgotten that.

It didnt matter anyway. If I had been a real artist, a painter or just sketching, the pencil out and getting that shape, the light at the window, her swaying there and on the window ledge the tall vase with the flowers, while the flowers, this bunch of flowers, the flowery bits spreading and drooping, only a few stalks till looking closely ye could see it was a bigger bunch, except the stalks were stuck together or so it looked to me, but what do I know, really, nothing, not about flowers and stalks. But that old song going through my brain, that would make anybody smile. Me too. She turned to do something, to walk somewhere, do something, to go and do something—and she saw me, saw me smiling, so she smiled too: a question.

No, I said, just eh … and that tune in my head that the way she looked was way beyond compare, that was how it was, when I saw her, just standing there, on the Sunday. That is how it was, by the window, the tenement across the road, the light and the old tree, her central to the image—so what this set up for me was that centrality, the external as well as internal, what could be seen through the glass as well as the objects within the room, the surroundings, the window frame and the end curtains,

and that was the Sunday, sure as God.

A Last Day

This was the day. This was today. When he woke up that morning he knew it for a fact. No matter what else, today was his last. He went for a piss, washed his hands and swallowed the clopidogrel, washed it down with a couple of mouthfuls of ice-cold water; fresh as the day is long. Thank god for water, he chortled, caught sight of his face in the mirror and paused, gazing at his eyes, not staring, just gazing. Thus the chortling belonged to the past. Was it his past? Today is

He did not finish the sentence. His eyelids had shut; we pull back the curtains. He glanced in and away from the mirror, his reflection, reflected being, oh god, the very last face on the very last day.

Not the last face on earth. Not at all. The last he wanted to see. He strode into the room and switched on the television.

The natural fish oils, no matter what, his grandpa always advocated the fish oils. They follow food, never in advance of food. Consuming the fish oils presupposes another day, another today.

This was the old folks. Thoughts of the day; one rises

On Becoming a Reader

; by rail daily to school, thus my penchant for departing
class prior to the schoolday's rightful conclusion that I
might not disintegrate through the unutterable boredom
of the subjects under consideration, my being forced to
consider these subjects that I might the better advance
beyond my fellows on the hierarchical ladder that was the
greatbritishsocialsystem, the place of my parents and family
not deemed of the lower orders but affixed therein through
no fault of our own howsomever the school subjects under
consideration purported to bring about the opportunity
of escape, nor yet the fault of my parents whose appar-
ent acceptance of this greatbritishsocialsystem ceded to
myself a marked nauseousness largely indescribable but by
authors whose ability to transcend that same indescriba-
bility by virtue of the act of storytelling exhibited not only
the sad limits of an inferior art but an open-armed adherence to that system, inducing within myself a consolidation
of purpose, effected by that same nauseousness, the predictable outcome of right reasoning, my unconscionable
assumption of the dubiety of all adult authority, my consequent contempt being ill-concealed, barely disguised,
leaving withdrawal from that society my only duty, the last
straw being the charred remains of a book I had purchased,
found in the fireplace, having been adjudged licentious by
my mother and set in flames, though the book were purchased on my own account by means of a monetary gift
from a grandmother, that was mine and mine alone to do as
wish should take me, so that now, approaching a birthdate

of more than passing interest its being the age by which a youth may decree that the departure of the education system is the one route by which the guarantee of sanity may be

of the spirit

I sit here you know I just sit here wondering what to do and my belly goes and my nerves are really on edge and I dont know what the fuck I'm to do it's something to think about I try to think about it while my head is going and sometimes this brings it back but only for a spell then suddenly I'm aware again of the feeling like a knife in the pit of my guts it's a worry I get worried about it because I know I should be doing things there are things needing doing I know I know I know it well but cant just bring myself to do them it isnt even as though there is that something that I can bring myself to do for if that was true it would be there I would be there and not having to worry about it at this stage my muscles go altogether and there's aches down the sides of my body they are actual aches and also under my arms at the shoulder my armpits there are aches and I think what I know about early-warning signs the early-warning signal of the dickey heart it feels like that is what it is the warning about impending strokes and death because also my chest is like that the pains at each side and stretching from there down the sides of my body as if I'm hunched right over the workbench with a case of snapped digestion the kind that has dissolved from the centre but still is there round the edges and I try to take myself out of it I think about a hundred and one things all different things different sorts of things the sorts of things you can think about as an average adult human being with an ordinary job and family the countless things and doing this can ease the aches for a time it can make me feel calm a bit as though things are coming under control due to thinking it all through as if really I am in control and able to consider things objectively as if I'm going daft or something but this is what it's like as if just my head's packed it in and I'm stranded there with this head full of nothing and with all that sort of dithering it'd make you think about you've got it so that sometimes I wish my hands were clamps like the kind joiners use and I could fasten them onto the sides of my head and then apply the thumbscrews so everything starts squeezing and squeezing

I try not to think about it too much because that doesnt pay you dont have to tell me I know it far too well already then I wouldnt be bothering otherwise I wouldnt be bothering but just sitting here and not bothering but just with my head all screwed up and not a single idea or thought but just maybe the aches and the pains, that physicality.

Wee Horrors

The backcourt was thick with rubbish as usual. What a mess. I never like thinking about the state it used to get into. As soon as a family flitted out to the new home all the weans were in and dragging off the abandoned furnishings & fittings, most of which they dumped. Plus with the demolition work going on you were getting piles of mortar and old brickwork everywhere. A lot of folk thought the worst kind of rubbish was the soft goods, the mattresses and dirty clothing left behind by the ragmen. Fleas were the problem. It seemed like every night of the week we were having to root them out once the weans came in. Both breeds we were catching, the big yins and the wee yins, the dark and the rusty brown. The pest-control went round from door to door. Useless. The only answer was keeping the weans inside but ours were too old for that. Having visitors in the house was an ordeal, trying to listen to what they were saying while watching for the first signs of scratching. Then last thing at night, before getting into bed, me and the wife had to make a point of checking through our own stuff. Apart from that there was little to be done about it. We did warn the weans but it was useless. Turn your back and they were off downstairs to play at wee houses, dressing-up in the clothes and bouncing on the mattresses till all you were left hoping was they would knock the stuffing out the fleas. Some chance. You have to drown the cunts or burn them. A few people get the knack of crushing them between thumbnail and forefinger but I could never master that. Anyway, fleas have got nothing to do with this. I was down in the backcourt to shout my pair up for their tea. The woman up the next close had told me they were all involved in some new den they had built and if I saw hers while I was at it I was to send them up right away. The weans were always making dens. It could be funny to see. You looked out the window and saw what you thought was a pile of rubble and maybe a sheet of tarpaulin stuck on the top. Take another look and you might see a wee head poking out, then another, and another, till finally maybe ten of them were standing there, thinking the coast was clear. But on this occasion I couldnt see a thing. I checked out most of the possibilities. Nothing. No signs of them anywhere. And it was quiet as well. Normally you would've at least heard a couple of squeaks. I tramped about for a time, retracing my steps and so on. I was not too worried. It would have been different if only my pair was missing but there was no sight nor sound of any description. And I was having to start considering the dunnies. This is where I got annoyed. I've always hated dunnies—pitchblack and that smell of charred rubbish, the broken glass, these things your shoes nudge against. Terrible. Then if you're in one and pause a moment there's this silence forcing you to listen. Really bad. I had to go down but. In the second one I tried I found some of the older mob, sitting in a kind of circle round two candles. They heard me come and I knew they had shifted something out of sight, but they recognised me okay and one of the lassies told me she had seen a couple of weans sneaking across to Greegor's. I was really angry at this. I had told them umpteen times never to go there. By rights the place should've got knocked down months ago but progress was being blocked for some reason I dont know, and now the squatters and a couple of the girls were in through the barricading. If you looked over late at night you could see the candle glow at the windows and during the day you were getting the cars crawling along near the pavement. It was hopeless. I went across. Once upon a time a grocer had a shop in the close and this had something to do with how it got called Greegor's. Judging from the smell of food he was still in business. At first I thought it was coming from up the close but the nearer I got I could tell it was coming from the dunny. Down I went. Being a corner block there were a good few twists and turns from the entrance lobby and I was having to go carefully. It felt like planks of wood I was walking on. Then the sounds. A kind of sizzling—making you think of a piece of fucking silverside in the oven, these crackling noises when the juice spurts out. Jesus christ. I shouted the names of my pair. The sound of feet scuffling. I turned a corner and got a hell of a shock—a woman standing in a doorway. Her face wasnt easy to see because of the light from behind her. Then a man appeared. He began nodding away with a daft smile on his face. I recognised them. Wineys. They had been dossing about the area for the past while. Even the face she had told a story, white with red blotches, eyes always seeming to water. She walked in this queer kind of stiff shuffle, her shoes flapping. When she stepped back from the doorway she drew the cuff of her coat sleeve across her mouth. The man was still giving his daft smiles. I followed. Inside the room all the weans were gathered round the middle of the floor. Sheets of newspaper had been spread about. I spotted my pair immediately—scared out their wits at seeing me. I just looked at them. Over at the fireplace a big fire was going, not actually in the fireplace, set to about a yard in front. The spit was fashioned above it and a wee boy stood there, he must've been rotating the fucking thing. Three lumps of meat sizzled away and just to the side were a few cooked bits lined in a row. I hadnt noticed the woman walk across but then she was there and making a show of turning the contraption just so I would know she wasnt giving a fuck about me being there. And him—still smiling, then beginning to make movements as if he wanted to demonstrate how it all worked. He was pointing out a row of raw lumps on the mantelpiece and then reaching for a knife with a thin blade. I shook my head, jesus christ right enough. I grabbed for my pair, yelling at the rest of the weans to get up that effing stair at once.

The Essence of Ignorance

When I first started in the job it was a better place to work. There was none of that fucking about that goes on nowadays. People would come in and do their bit and then that was it, off they would go. Nowadays they seem to want things all their own way. I'm not against progress, it just worries me the way they go about it. Sometimes I feel certain things have got to be said and to hell if people dont want to listen and one of these things I'm talking about is to do with the working man—in a nutshell, the working man isnt ready to take over the reins. As simple as that. The trouble is if you stand up and be counted you wind up getting attacked for it. If people dont agree then well and good but they should be prepared to speak out instead of just shouting you down. I was at the branch meeting the other day and when the floor was available and I started to talk somebody burst out laughing, sarcastic and totally false, and done intentionally to make a fool of me, to make me a laughing stock. Maybe I am a laughing stock but what I say is what I say and I should be able to say it at a branch meeting and if I cant then the membership needs to be told why. I lost my temper because of it and made a mess of what I wanted to say. That was the worst it. That was why that fellow laughed in the first place, so I couldn't be heard. It was my argument he didnt want people to hear and the question has to be asked "why?" Everybody started talking at the one time and half of them were losing their temper and the other half were just laughing. So nothing got done, and it is obvious to me that nothing will get done. Tam that works along from me, he agrees with a lot of what I say. Maybe not everything but most of it. He was telling me about his own experiences and some of it is horrible and makes your blood boil. He never goes to any meetings nowadays. He calls them a rabble. You can see his point but if we all did the same then nothing would get done at all. I am not saying all what goes on at branch meetings is rubbish; there can be some good points raised. But if the working man ran the country the way he runs his branch meetings then all I can say is look out. Some of them are real left wing lefties and think they can just take over the reins and all's well that ends well. They dont realise the slightest wee bit about the goings on involved. If you ask them about the Stock Market they can only hum and haw but the reality is they don't know a damn thing about it. They think everything works by itself. If they take over the government everything just carries on as you were, the only difference being that people start earning a fair crack of the whip. It is nonsense. You try to tell them and they dont listen, they dont want to hear, they turn round and tell ye ye dont know what ye're talking about. They do but you dont. They start shouting about the means to production and if ye ask them what they mean they cant tell ye except they think everything will sort itself out, and what I say is who by? Who is it going to sort it out? Somebody has to. Oh well we'll figure that out later. That is what one of them said. The one thing I knew there was he was a single man with no family to take care of. The essence of ignorance. You cant just sit back and expect it to all turn out right. You have to start thinking about how it will happen and how to make it happen. If ye dont do that ye're in trouble. That's what I believe and I dont mind saying it.

Cute Chick!

There used to be this talkative old lady with a polite English accent who roamed the betting shops of Glasgow being avoided by everybody. In those far-off days nay receipts were given when ye made a bet. Ye wrote it out on a slip of paper and added yer nom-de-plume at the bottom. Yer nom-de-plume was the name ye used for identification purposes. Most guys did variations on their birthdates and the initials of their name. If ye backed a winner and went to get paid ye would whisper it to the settler at the pay-out window, keeping it a secret between you and him. That old English lady but she didnay care who heard. Whenever she appeared the heavily backed favourite was about to get beat by a big outsider, and there she was, crying out in this surprised way about how she had managed to choose the winner, before going to collect her dough at the pay-out window. When the settler asked for her nom-de-plume she spoke loudly and clearly: Cute Chick!

It made the punters' blood run cold.

Our Times

There was this upper-middle-class fellow who was a genuine goody. Charles was his name. He may have been called after the English monarch. He was a boring individual in adult company but children suffered him and allowed him to join their games. I did not know him personally and might have thought highly of him if I had. I shall never know. On the whole his entire life was boring insofar as anyone's life is boring. But this is hearsay.

Charles had a full-time upper-middle-class type of job. At the same time he was a complete individual, a whole human being, figuratively. So too was Sian, his wife. Sian is an unusual name for a woman which was of additional interest to myself, as is the Gàidhlig tradition.

Charles and Sian shared an interest in the musical arts and were at ease in their own community. This appealed to me. She was of the middling middle-class; a girl who, prior to the first pregnancy, held a responsible position in a local law firm. She would pick up her career where she had left off. Once her youngest child reached nursery-school age, she hoped. Sian was counting the months.

Theirs were decent children, neither stuck-up nor namby-pamby. They did not feel ill at ease if adults were in the same room yet had their own little circle of friends. They made no attempt to dominate mixed-age companies. Charles was proud of that. He disliked children being pushed to the fore in adult society. He thought it demeaning.

Sian thought the same but in her it occasioned pangs of guilt. In a curious way she was proud of that guilt, yet kept it to herself. Thus the guilt was a secret and she disliked secrets. She found them perplexing. One evening, before switching off the light, she looked into her eyes in the dressing table mirror. Soon after she joined Charles in bed. She blurted out the secret to Charles. Had he heard? His only reply was a silence but with the strong possibility that he had smiled. Sian sensed as much. She liked his smile. It was beautiful. Oddly, it was their daughter who inherited the smile. Sian wished it were the boy. His had reminded her of her own father for whom she had never much cared, but that of his memory, the smile of his memory, the smile of his memory.

Sian thought thoughts suggesting other modes were possible, modes of life, modes of moving; perhaps, but not of loving. She loved Charles.

Twice a year they and the children holidayed together. These were not unadventurous forays and in retrospect enjoyed thoroughly. During these moments, Charles and Sian thought to sell up and move abroad should the opportunity present itself. If such might occasion the future would reveal.

News of Charles and Sian reached us through neighbours. Each time I encountered these neighbours it was not a reminder but a rejoinder. We were not close and never would become so. It is true to state, nevertheless, that the drama had yet to begin.

Bangs & a Full Moon

A fine Full Moon from the third storey through the red reflection from the city lights: this was the view. I gazed at it, lying outstretched on the bed-settee. I was thinking arrogant thoughts of that, Full Moons, and all those awful fucking writers who present nice images in the presupposition of universal fellowship under the western Stars when all of a sudden: BANG, an object hurtling out through the window facing mine across the street.

The windows on this side had been in total blackness; the building was soon to be demolished and formally uninhabited.

BANG. An object hurtled through another window. No lights came on. Nothing could be seen. Nobody was heard. Down below the street was deserted; broken glass glinted. I returned to the bed-settee and when I had rolled the smoke, found I already had one smouldering in the ashtray. I got back up again and closed the curtains. I was writing in pen & ink so not to waken the kids and wife with the banging of this machine I am now using.

George Taggart's Bottom

Halt! Go no further or I shall shoot you dead! commanded the icy cold figure who stepped out from the shadows with a sadistic, and characteristic but malevolent calm. Old-Etonian George Taggart stopped in his tracks when he heard the accented vowels of the cold-hearted killer. The former CIA-SAS operative stared at the foreign personage with steely determination and cool disdain. Out of the corner of his eye he saw that his gaudily uniformed adversary held a fully loaded XXG 92 breech-based repeater-kill blunderbuss. Instantly George Taggart recognised this horrible weapon from direct experience gained from his own personal career choice, having been a foremost specialist in firearm reconnaissance while on temporary assignment to the regimental bodyguard of the dashing young King Arrivahbi, absolute monarch of a benign friendly power who were slowly developing their pro-democracy outlook. At once George Taggart guessed with appropriate precision that this highly developed instrument of mass murder had been manufactured in the vast ironworks of north-eastern Siberia. Suddenly, no sooner had he thought the thought itself, than the former CIA-SAS operative had that horrible instrument of inhuman horrors thrust into his face and though of stalwart fortitude, he stumbled bravely backwards and landed on his muscular bottom, cracking both cheek bones badly and severely on the icy cold concrete floor of the dingy dark dungeon in the depth of the communist stronghold which had once been a castle with manicured lawns and exquisite parquetry in the fashion of Faberge, a generation or two earlier, in the time of the old Czar and Czarina but which had been taken away by its more recent terrorist insurgents who didn't give tuppence for all the fine arts of yesteryear, and now the luckless but heroic old-Etonian, George Taggart, had suffered the consequences.

Governor of the Situation

I hate this part of the city—the stench of poverty, violence, decay, death; the things you usually discern in suchlike places. I dont mind admitting I despise the poor with an intensity that surprises my superiors. But they concede to me on most matters. I am the acknowledged governor of the situation. I'm in my early thirties. Hardly an ounce of spare flesh hangs on me—I'm always on the go—nervous energy—because my appetite is truly gargantuan. For all that, I've heard it said on more than one occasion that my legs are like hollow pins.

Leather Jacket

Guilt's aye personal.
What ye talking about?
See you're okay because you've got a good leather jacket.
What you want me to feel guilty about it?
...
What's funny?
...
Eh?
...
What's funny?
Nothing.
So what ye laughing about?
I'm no laughing. I'm just no going to feel guilty about it.
Sure, okay, it's a personal decision.
What ...
It's a personal decision.
What's a personal decision?
Guilt.
Guilt. I dont feel guilt—guilty, I dont feel it.
Personal decisions, they're personal. I'm talking if one person makes it as opposed to a committee. Although committees are made up of people anyway, I'm talking individuals and personalities, et cetera. But if one person makes it ...
What ye talking about?
...
Eh?
Any tissues?

Naw.

Fucking nose man jesus fuck—cold innit.

Aye.

I dont fancy wearing the skins of dead animal but, definitely not.

Hide.

Hide yeh, I wouldnay wear that man.

...

What time is it now?

Fuck knows.

Fucking dead animals man.

I know the arguments.

I know you know the arguments.

Aye well ...

I've no even got a smoke, have you?

Naw, that evil bastard man he used them for his ayn fucking shit then hardly gave us a drag.

Bastard.

...

...

I know ye know the arguments man so dont fucking, know what I mean, laying that at my door, fuck that man—I bought it down the market man she bought it for me and it was secondhand. Alright?

...

Alright?

Yeah yeah, sorry, it's just like ...

What?

...

What?

It's just how some people think like if ye know them man like it's a way to get rid of the guilt.

You've got guilt on the fucking brain.

Oh I'm guilty I'm guilty and then ye dont have to do fuck all, that's the craic man with them. Know what I mean, a fucking course of action instead of just talking. What do ye call it, absolving the guilt man that's you absolving the guilt.

Yeah. I knew that anyway, it was secondhand, I knew it.

Well so dont give us any crap then man if that's what ye're giving us.

I'm no giving ye any crap man.

Well dont.

. . .

Time is it now?

Fucking bastard, where the hell is he?

How the fuck do I know, never tells me fuck all.

Cronies

For three long days and three long nights we drank together, me being there simply because I had nowhere else to go, nobody else to be with, not a soul, not in the whole world; and the other strictly because it was business, and the business lay in the undermining of the other, his crony, me. And not that he was going anywhere either as it happens, although this information is irrelevant, him being a sort of a businessman first but a human being second, and the business in hand was in being here with me, his crony, so-called.

The rest of the company found the thing a spectacle, an incident worthy of the greatest attention. On the one hand it was amusing but on the other there was this sordid undercurrent, them being in the know about the nature of the business. But me and him, as far as ordinary onlookers were concerned, we were the greatest of pals, even if it now seems likely we neither of us understood one word the other was saying.

There was something about it all made the rest of the company wax lyrical, a bad sweet kind of thing. You would have thought the one was not being undermined by the other, that this other was not in the business of undermining me. But the real reason for this false lyricism lay in the rest of the company wanting to consolidate their own fraternity. And meanwhile this barely disguised actual assault on fraternity was continuing right in front of their very eyes, it was quite disgusting, it just deserved contempt, the strong one seeking out the intimacy of the weaker, i.e.

me. Plus over their bottles of beer and tumblers of whisky or vodka.

Then it became noticeable he was drawing in for the final assault, his friendliness was gradually being thrown off for the disguise it was, not so much in any outward display of violence but in an absentmindedness that accompanied each one of his actions. It was almost as though he who was to be undermined, and I mean by that myself, that I had become a habit, one more habit, of a tired business-man, if you could call him that; speaking personally I would say he was just an inveterate snob, and that was how he adopted such a nomenclature; the truth is he wasnt a real businessman. He was playing a double game. In the first place he wanted not to be seen as a businessman since most of his associates and acquaintances were socialists or if not socialists as such at least were all in hostile positions toward reactionaries or toryness or whatever, shade or hue. But then again in the second place he wanted everybody to secretly think of him as a businessman, maybe subcon-sciously; and that because to be a businessman was to be in a position of power.

And above all this was his real goal, power, as witness his assault on myself, someone the world presumed to be an old and trusted crony.

The day the company finally shattered began from him entering the room and the victim, myself, already seated at the table, rising to not so much greet him as wave him into the empty seat facing me. But he just stared at me and he grinned, and when he grinned it was a horror because it was so internalised. I read the signs and I was greatly taken aback, I gaped up at the ceiling as if I was looking for a religious emblem but the rest of the company, they were staring really hostilely at me and I couldnt fathom it out. You have to remember that until the businessman's strong interest they had been more than willing to abuse me for a scapegoat, more than willing, and at this moment there was nothing quite so obvious. I wanted to shout to them about how it had all happened only in this short span of time, how three long days and nights were so short. It was a mortifying experience and it was me that was the martyr.

The Later Transgression

At this stage, when things appeared to be running smoothly, his transgression surprised me. Upon reflection it was no more and no less than I should have anticipated. His life may have been seen as one to emulate, to strive after or towards, but it was far from commendable. I knew that. He had not lived a perfect life. My friends respected him; young men like ourselves. It is safe to say that.

A companion of ours, a musician, did not survive though his existence exhausted itself in a similar way. When we three were together and smiling on how things had been, partly it was relief that we had survived at all. None among us pretended, none among us was the hypocrite.

In the ordinary ethical sense we had not lived just lives but nor had we pretensions toward the religious or theological sense of other existences, nor of existences yet to come. For myself I had no intentions of accepting a second existence. I grew weary of Lives to Come, a Life to Come, that Life to Come. As with our former friend I was one of many, content that those who follow should wield the baton.

Universals do not exist. There is no ethic, no code of morality, no moral sense at the inner depth of our being. From an early period I too was aware that the sensibility is unaffected by the violence or abuses perpetrated by one on another, even if the one is close to us. Yet I was perceived as ruthless. So too was our former friend. But did he fully understand what ruthlessness might amount to? Perhaps he did. When his grandfather died he rowed the boat that carried his ashes. His father and younger brother were seated at the stern. His younger brother unscrewed the receptacle and emptied the ashes midway across. His father could have stopped him. The following is hearsay, that he too could have stopped him.

                    Dear
                  o dear o
                  dear. And
                 yet she must
                have been near
                about 30 years
                 of age. But
                 a certain
                    pair
                 of legs have
                the following
               shape: slim over
               the knees with the
              sloped move down to
              the ankles which arent
             thick. She was wearing a
            miniskirt, and orange hair
             with rollers stuck in; about
  5'6"   in her red heels. And
  this   voice of an amazing
  kind   of hoarseness when
  first   I heard her in the
  shop   at the corner while
  she   asked for a pound
  of   brown sugar and 20
  of   your kingsize tips
  and   a box of cadbury's
  as   well Archie if you
            dont mind. And pushing
            out through the door
            she let it swing back
            as if leaving it for
            me. Against the wall
            of her close she
            was leaning as I
            walked by clutch-
            ing my golden vir-
            ginia. And at 23
            years of age I was
            going through a bad
            patch with the
                wife but
                I did go
                on past.
                A couple
                of days
                later I
                saw her
                in the
                street
                bawling
            at   some
            old   timer:
            Ya   manky
            auld swine
            ye!   You
            still owe
            two   quid
            from last
                week.

Manchester in July

I was there once without enough for a room, not even for a night's lodgings in the local Walton House. 6/6d it was at the time which proves how fucking recent it was. At the NAB a clerk proffered a few bob as a temporary measure and told me to come back once I had fixed myself up with a rentbook. I got irritated at this because of the logical absurdity but they were not obliged to dish out cash to people without addresses. By the time I had worked out my anger I was skint again (ten fags and some sort of basic takeaway from a Chinese Restaurant). I wound up trying for a kip in the station, then tramped about the 'dilly trying to punt the wares to Mr and Mrs Anybody. When it was morning I headed along and under the bridge to Salford, eventually picking up another few bob in the office across from Strangeways. I went away back there and then and booked in at the Walton for that coming evening, just to be on the safe side.

The middle of July. What a wonderful heat it was. I spent most of the day snoozing full stretch on my back in a grass square adjacent to the House, doing my best to conserve the rest of the bread.

Into the communal lounge about 6:30 p.m. I sat on this ancient leather effort of a chair which had brass studs stuck in it. The other seating in the place was similarly odd and disjointed. Old guys sprawled everywhere snoring and farting and burping and staring in a glassy-eyed way at the television. I had been scratching myself as soon as I crossed the threshold, just at the actual idea of it. Yet in a funny fucking way it was quite comfortable and relaxing and it seemed to induce in you a sort of stupor. Plus it was fine getting the chance to see a telly again. One felt like a human being. I mind it was showing The Fugitive with that guy David Janssen and this tall police lieutenant who was chasing him about the States (and wound up he was the guy who killed Janssen's wife). I was right into it anyway, along with the remaining few in the room who were still compos mentis, when in walks these three blokes in clean boilersuits and they switched it off, the telly. Ten minutes before the end or something. I jumped out the chair and stood there glaring at them. A couple of the old guys got up then; but they just headed off towards the door, and then upstairs to the palliasses. It was fucking bedtime! 10:50 p.m. on a Thursday night. It might even have been a fucking Friday.

That Other

The people filed into the Memorial Tower in some consternation for the culprit was still at the gate, still shrieking that horrific blasphemy.

And all the while the foolish inconsistency prevailed.

Of those involved only two individuals could even hope to be aware of its singular significance. Yet the people were now spiralling upwards, blinking.

The Habits of Rats

This part of the factory had always been full of rats. It was the storeroom. Large piles of boxes were stacked at the bottom end while scattered about the floor was all manner of junk. Here in particular dwelled the rats. They came out at night. During the nightshift one man had charge of the storeroom; he was always pleased when somebody called up with an order and stayed for a chat. His office lay at the opposite end of the storeroom. He would keep all the lights on here but leave the bottom end in darkness, unless being obliged to go down to collect a box from stock, in which case he switched on every light in the entire place to advise the rats of his approach.

One night a gaffer phoned him on the intercom and told him to get such and such a box and deliver it immediately to the machineshop. Now the storeman had been halfway through the first of his cheese sandwiches at the time but the interruption did not annoy him. There was little work to keep his mind occupied during the night; he was always glad of the opportunity to wander round the factory pushing his wheelbarrow.

Once he had all the lights on at the bottom end he found himself to be holding his parcel of cheese sandwiches. Stuffing the remainder of the one he had been eating straight into his mouth he laid the parcel down on a box so that he could manoeuvre the requisitioned box onto the wheelbarrow. He pushed it along to the exit. He switched off the lights as he went. Outside the storeroom he halted. He dashed back inside and switched them on again and quickly went down to retrieve the sandwiches before the rats could gobble them all up. In his office he placed the parcel on top of a filing cabinet.

He enjoyed the wander, stopping off here and there for a smoke or a chat with particular people he was friendly with. Back in the storeroom he brewed a fresh pot of tea and sat down to continue his lunchbreak. He only ate two of the sandwiches.

Later on in the night a gaffer phoned him with another requisition. He phoned back after when again there was no reply. Eventually he came round in person, to discover the storeman lying on the floor in a coma. He had the storeman rushed off to hospital at once.

For a fortnight the storeman remained in this coma. They took out all of his blood and filled him up with other blood. They said that a rat, or rats, had urinated on his sandwiches and thus had his entire blood system been poisoned.

The storeman said he could remember a slight dampness about the sandwiches he had eaten, but that they had definitely not been soggy. He reckoned the warmth of his office may have dried them out a bit. He said when he left them lying on the box he must have forgotten to close the parcel properly. But he was only gone moments. He could not understand it at all. After his period of convalescence they transferred him to a permanent job on the dayshift, across in the machineshop.

The Melveille Twins, page 82

The long feud between the Melveille Twins was resolved by a duel in which stipulations of rather obvious significance had been laid down, the two men were bound back to back by a length of thick hemp knotted round their waists. Having gained choice of weapon the elder had already decided upon the cutlass and insofar as the younger is noted as having been "corrie-fistit," to infer a hint of possible irony may not be misguided.* Few events of a more bloodthirsty nature are thought to have occasioned in the country of Scotland.

When the handkerchief fell the slashing began; within moments the lower part of each body was running red with blood. While wielding the weapon each held the empty hand aloft as though unwilling so much as to even touch the other. Eventually the small group of men silently observing made their way off from the scene—a scene that for them had soon proved sour.

Only one man remained. He seems to have been a servant of some sort but little is known of his history aside from the fact of his being fairly literate.

The affair appeared at an end when the elder twin stumbled and together they landed on the ground. But almost immediately each had rolled in such a manner they were lying on the hands that grasped the weapons: for a brief period they kicked at each other. Coming to them with

---

* To be "corrie-fistit" in certain parts of Scotland is to be left-handed, even in the present day.

a jug of fresh water and strips of a clean material, the man bathed their wounds. He then lifted and placed the weapons outwith their arms' reach; he departed at this point. Whether the actual duel ended here is an open question. We are only certain that the feud ceased.

le joueur

Him with the long face and that conical hat sitting there with the clay pipe stuck in his mouth, the widower: he enters this café around 7 every evening with a nod to the barman, a quick look to ensure his chair and table are vacant; though in a place as quiet as this anything else seems out of the question. Lurking about at the rear of the table is a wee black & white dog that finally settles into a prone position in the shadows by the wall beneath the grimy mirror. On putting the tall bottle of wine and the two glasses down onto the table, the widower has tugged this huge coloured handkerchief from his right jacket pocket, and into it has given a muffled honk; and sniffed while stuffing it back out of sight. Several moments on he is glancing across at the clock on the gantry and taking the handkerchief out once more, to wipe at his nostrils.

The door has opened.

That younger man—him with the upturned brim on his hat— has walked in, hands in coat pockets; and a half twitch of the head by way of greeting the barman; and a half rise of the eyebrows on seeing the widower's glance at the clock. A deck of cards he lifts from the bar en route to the empty seat facing the widower. With a slow yawn the dog lowers its head, closes its eyes, reverting into its prone position. While the wine is being poured by one the other is shuffling to deal methodically, ten cards apiece.

Later, him with the conical hat will rise and knock the bowl of the clay pipe against the heel of his right boot and without so much as a grunt will head for the exit followed by the wee black & white dog; and this dog must dodge smartly to get out before the door shuts on it.

That younger man will have refilled his own glass and will then gather up the cards and, as he is shuffling, he will be gazing round the interior of the room: but the only person present apart from the barman will be Paul Cézanne: and so he will continue to shuffle the cards for a period, before setting out the first game of solitaire while half wondering if his kids are behaving themselves.

Busted Scotch

I had been looking forward to this Friday night for a while. The first wage from the first job in England. The workmates had assured me they played Brag in this club's casino. It would start when the cabaret ended. Packed full of bodies inside the main hall; rows and rows of men-only drinking pints of bitter and yelling at the strippers. One of the filler acts turned out to be a scotchman doing this harry-lauder thing complete with kilt and trimmings. A terrible disgrace. Keep Right On To The End Of The Road he sang with four hundred and fifty males screaming Get Them Off Jock. Fine if I had been drunk and able to join in on the chants but as it was I was staying sober for the Brag ahead. Give the scotchman his due but—he stuck it out till the last and turning his back on them all he gave a big boo boopsi-doo with the kilt pulled right up and flashing the Y-fronts. Big applause he got as well. The next act on was an Indian Squaw. Later I saw the side door into the casino section opening. I went through. Blackjack was the game until the cabaret finished. I sat down facing a girl around my own age, she was wearing a black dress cut off the shoulders. Apart from me there was no other punters in the room.

Want to start, she asked.

Aye. Might as well. I took out my wages.

O, you're scotch. One of your countrymen was on stage tonight.

That a fact.

She nodded as she prepared to deal. She said, How much are you wanting to bet?

I shrugged. I pointed to the wages lying there on the edge of the baize.

All of it ...

Aye. The lot.

She covered the bet after counting what I had. She dealt the cards.

Twist.

Bust ...

not too long from now tonight will be that last time

He was walking slowly. His pace quickened then slackened once more. He stopped by the doorway of a shop and lighted a cigarette. The floor was dry, a sort of parquetry. He lowered himself down to sit on his heels, his arms folded, elbows resting on his knees, his back to the glass door.

He could have gone straight home and crept inside and into bed perhaps quietly enough not to disturb her and come morning, maybe that hour earlier than usual, and out and away, before she was awake. But why bother. He could simply not return. In this way they would simply not meet, they would not have to meet. And that would be great. He was not up to it. It was not something he felt capable of managing. It was not something he was capable of. He could not cope with it.

But why bother. If he was obliged to do certain things and then failed to do these things then that was that and nothing could be offered instead. He had always known the truth of that. Always; even though he seemed never to have given it voice. Never; especially not with her. She would never have understood.

And then there were his silences. That inability he had to get out of himself. It was not disgust, not contempt; nothing like that. It was something different altogether. But he had no wish to work out what the hell it was.

He had been trying to adapt for years. And now she was there now lying in bed sleeping or awake, about to become awake, to peer at the clockface, knowing she is not as warm as usual, because of course he is not home yet and the time, and her eyes.

He keeps imagining going somewhere else and taking a room perhaps with full board in some place far away where all the people are just people, people he does not know and has no obligation to speak to. There was something good about that. He inhaled on the cigarette then raised himself up and bent his knees a couple of times, before pacing on. After a time he slowed, but was soon walking more quickly.

Good Intentions

We had been sceptical from the very outset but the way he set about the tasks suited us perfectly. In fact, it was an eye-opener. He would stand there with the poised rifle, the weather-beaten countenance, the shiny little uniform; yet giving absolutely nothing away. His legs were bandy and it produced a swaggering stance, as though he had no time for us and deep down regarded us as amateurs. But we, of course, made no comment. The old age pensioner is a strange beast on occasion and we were well acquainted with this, perhaps too well acquainted. In the final analysis it was probably that at the root of the project's failure.

A Rolling Machine

Sandy had been leading me around all morning in a desire to impress—to interest me in him and in this place where he earned his living, also to show his workmates that here he was with his very own learner. He explained various workings and techniques of the machines and asked if I had any queries but not to worry if I didnt because at this stage it was unlikely though I would soon become familiar with it all, just so long as I took it easy and watched everything closely. Gradually he was building to the climax of his own machine. Here I was to learn initially. Up and down he strode patting its parts and referring to it as her and she as if it was a bus or an old-fashioned sailing ship. She wont let you down Jimmy is the sort of stuff he was giving me. The machine was approximately twenty-five feet in length and was always requiring attention from the black squad; but even so, it could produce the finest quality goods of the entire department when running to her true form. Placing me to the side in such a way that I could have an unrestricted view he kicked her off. He was trying hard not to look too pleased with himself. Every now and then he shifted stance to ensure I was studying his movements. His foot was going on the pedal while his right hand was holding the wooden peg-like instrument through which he played the coiled wire between the middle and forefingers of his left hand out onto the rolling section of the appara-tus. At one point he turned to make a comment but a knot had appeared on the wire, jamming on the wooden instrument and ripping off the top end of his thumb while the machine continued the rolling operation and out of the fleshy mess spiralled a hair-thin substance like thread being unrolled from a bobbin somewhere inside the palm, and it was running parallel to the wire from the coil. Sandy's eyes were gazing at me in a kind of astonished embarrassment until eventually he collapsed, just a moment before one of his workmates elbowed me clear in order to reach the trip-safety-rail.

Foreign language users

A wise man resists playing cards with foreign language users. This is a maxim Mister Joseph Kerr always should have been well aware. So how come he had succumbed to temptation yet again? Because he thought he would take them, that's how. If you had discussed the point prior to play he would have nodded in a perfunctory fashion—that's how much a part of him the maxim was. And yet he still succumbed. Of course. Gamblers are a strange breed. In fact, when he noticed his pockets were empty he frowned. That is exactly what he did, he frowned. Then he stared at the foreign language users who by this time had forgotten all about him. And the croupier was shuffling the deck for a new deal. And yes, she too was concealing her impatience in an unsubtle way, this croupier, and this unsubtlety was her method of displaying it, her impatience.

Mister Joseph Kerr nudged the spectacles up his nose a wee bit, a nervous gesture. His chair moved noisily, causing the other players to glance at him.

But what was he to do now? There was nothing he could do now. No, nothing to be done. It was something he just had to face. And yet these damn foreign language users had taken his money by devices one could scarcely describe as being other than less than fair, not to put too fine a point on things. And how in the name of all that's holy could the fact that it was himself to blame be of any consolation?

He scratched his ear and continued to stand there, by the chair, and then he sighed in an exaggerated manner but it was bitterly done, and he declared how things had gone too far for him now, that he had so to speak come to the end of his tether. The croupier merely looked at him in reply but this look might well have been a straightforward appeal for a new player.

Mister Joseph Kerr shrugged. Then he stood to the side, making space for the new player who moved easily onto the seat. There was a pause. Mister Joseph Kerr had raised his eyebrows in a slightly mocking fashion. He smiled at the new player and touched him on the shoulder, saying how he should definitely pay heed to that which he knew so thoroughly beforehand. The new player glared at the hand on his shoulder. What is the meaning of this? he murmured.

In all probability he too was a foreign language user. Mister Joseph Kerr nodded wearily. Maybe he was just bloody well growing old! Could that be it? He sighed as he strolled round the table, continuing on in the style of somebody heading to an exit. He entered the gents' washroom and gazed at himself in the mirror. It was a poor show right enough, this tired face he saw; and something in it too as if, as if his eyes, had his eyes perhaps clouded over ... but of course his spectacles, having misted over. The thought how at least he was breathing, at least he was breathing, that was worth remembering.

More complaints from the American Correspondent

Jesus christ man this tramping from city to city—terrible. No pavements man just these back gardens like you got to walk right down by the edge of the road man and them big fucking doberman pinschers they're coming charging straight at you. Then the ghettos for christ sake you got all them mothers lining the streets man they're tugging at your sleeves, hey you, gies a bite of your cheeseburger. Murder polis.

Benson's Visitor

Every Sunday afternoon he appeared. The patient who had the first bed on the left at the ward entrance always heralded his arrival with the cry: It's Benson's visitor! But he never acknowledged this cry. He was aware some might think him deaf. He stood on the threshold peering down both sides of the ward for ten to fifteen seconds, perhaps to see if Benson was still there and if so whether he had been shifted to a different bed as sometimes happened. If everything was as it should be he stared at the highly polished floor and walked steadily down the right-hand passage, to the bottom end, and from there across to Benson's bed at the end of the left-hand row. At the beginning he had nodded and occasionally greeted other patients but over the years he had ceased doing this and nowadays he could scarcely bear to look at patients other than Benson. And if Benson was awake he found it increasingly difficult to look at him. He used to smile in a friendly manner at the nurses but they barely noticed his presence. If ever he put a question such as Not so good today, is he? the most they would give was a yes or no but sometimes not even that, as if they had not heard him speak at all even. The new nurses were better but gradually they became used to things and acted no differently from the others. Hardly anyone else ever visited the ward and those who did seldom stayed for more than quarter of an hour and they spent most of that gazing vacantly about the ward. On occasion they would stare across as though looking at Benson whereas it seemed obvious they were looking at his visitor. There was one time Benson's visitor saw somebody leave an article on the chair beside the bed of the patient he had been sitting at. He was not sure what to do about it. Eventually, after the person had departed, he walked across and uplifted the article and quickly rushed out to return it. But the person acted in a peculiar way and pretended not to recognise the object. Benson's visitor took it into the Sister's office and attempted to explain what had happened but the Sister was impatient and did not show any interest in the matter at all. She waved him away. He put the article back onto the chair and tried not to think about it. Next Sunday of course the chair was empty and no-one ever referred to either it or the incident ever again. This was many months ago, prior to the arrival of the patient on the left at the ward entrance. And yet, there was something about this patient that made Benson's visitor think that he knew of the affair.

Benson had been a member of the ward longer than anyone else. His visitor accompanied the wheelchair that transported him there. Although the nurse had observed him following she said nothing, merely indicated a large placard pinned to the wall. The placard gave the visiting times. Benson's visitor stared at it for a long while, until the sound of the creaking wheelchair had died away. He missed the subsequent Sunday because of it. It was a feeling he had not cared for.

This afternoon Benson lay snoring fitfully but peacefully. His visitor stared at the slack mouth and the way the chin drooped. When the bell rang Benson's eyes opened. The gaze settled on his visitor who hastily looked down at the floor. Benson's head began to move back and forth against the piled pillows as though to alleviate an itch. His eyes remained on his visitor for a period, then they closed. His visitor's sigh was quite audible. After a moment he stooped to lift his hat and shabby briefcase from where they had been lying. Across the way an older nurse arranged flowers in a vase. She did not notice his approach. He moved to the right side of her at the precise second she moved to the left. He hesitated and she turned swiftly and strode along and out of the ward. There were no other people about except patients and they all seemed to be sleeping. Then another visitor appeared in the doorway. Benson's visitor returned slowly to where he had been sitting and he returned the briefcase and hat to where they had been lying, and he sat down carefully. Shortly afterwards he was aware of a muffled conversation coming from somewhere to his rear but he was not able to look round to see. A voice called: It's Benson's visitor! and gave an abrupt laugh.

He stared at the floor for a long time. Gradually he wanted to see what was happening around him and he raised his head. But Benson stared at him. Benson glowered. Who are you? he groaned.

His visitor smiled weakly.

I dont know you.

His visitor inclined his head and stared at the floor beneath the bed.

Is he visiting me? groaned Benson. I dont know him from Adam!

Footsteps approached. He estimated at least two people.

I dont know him. Who is he? Who are you? cried Benson.

Two nurses were looking at his visitor and he smiled faintly at them. Not so good today, is he? His heart thumped.

The nurses looked at the patient with concern and one of them said: Oh he's your visitor.

His visitor nodded his head but without daring to look at the elderly man in the bed. But Benson cried, I dont know him from Adam. Why is he sitting there? I dont want him sitting there. He's like old Father Time!

The older nurse smiled down on him. Come now, what a thing to say! You mustnt embarrass your visitor.

He is your visitor! smiled the younger nurse.

Who is he? groaned Benson, attempting to raise himself up by the elbows as though for a fuller look at him. But the older nurse snapped:

Come along now lie down!

The patient lay back down immediately and stared sideways away from both his visitor and the two nurses, the younger of whom glanced at her colleague and then said to Benson's visitor, Who are you? And she smiled as though to soften matters.

Benson's visitor jumped. Somebody else had arrived suddenly. It was the Sister.

Benson's visitor . . . began the younger nurse.

Of course its Benson's visitor, she said, What's going on here?

Who is he? murmured Benson.

Oh you know fine well, replied the Sister.

Who are you? Benson groaned.

His visitor smiled at the Sister. He wondered whether the other visitor and any of the patients were listening. He thought he should say something. He cleared his throat but was not able to speak. At last he managed: Not so good.

The Sister was speaking in a low unhurried voice to the two nurses who responded as to a direct command, but none noticed Benson's gasp, and his eyelids closed.

The older nurse said to his visitor, You better go now, visiting's over.

He nodded and gripped his hat and briefcase, got off the chair and walked from the ward without glancing back. Out along the lengthy corridor the younger nurse appeared from behind a pillar. Are you a relative? she asked.

You must have a record, he said.

Come along now you wont be on it. You wont be there. She shook her head at him.

A wave of nausea hit him and he wanted down onto the floor, down onto the floor until it passed. Somebody was holding him by the arm. It was the other nurse, and behind her stood the other patient with a worried frown on his forehead. His hat and briefcase were leaving him, the hat having fallen perhaps but the briefcase from out of his hand. And the younger nurse steadied him. Come along now, she was saying.

The older nurse smiled. That's the ticket, she said.

learning the Story

I once met an old lady sitting under a bridge over the River Kelvin. She smoked Capstan full-strength cigarettes and played the mouthorgan.

The moon was well up as I had passed along the footpath listening to the water fall at the small dam beyond the old mill. Aye, cried the voice, you are there are you! If I had spotted her before she had me I would have crept back the way I had come. Aye, she cried again. And rising to her feet she brought out the mouthorgan from somewhere inside the layers of her clothing, and struck up the tune: Maxwelton Braes Are Bonny was the name of it. Halfway through she suddenly stopped and she stared at me and grunted something. She sat down again on the damp grass with her back against the wall at the tunnel entrance; she stared at her boots. Very good that, I said to her. From her shopping bag she pulled out the packet of Capstan full-strength cigarettes. She sniffed. And I felt as if I had let her down. I always liked that tune, I told her. She struck a match and lighted a cigarette. She flicked the match a distance and it landed with smoke still rising from it. Drawing the shopping bag in between her raised knees she inhaled deeply, exhaled staring at her boots. Cheerio then, I said. I paced on beneath the bridge aware of my footsteps echoing.

The old lady wore specs and had a scarf wrapped round her neck. Her nose was bony. Her skirt may have showed under the hem of her coat. When she was playing the mouthorgan she had moved slightly from foot to foot. Her coat was furry.

First Stroke

The old woman opened her eyes when the gas-light flickered, but soon closed them again. The boy was squinting at the football news on the back page, trying to find something new to read. He let the newspaper fall onto his lap and lifted the tongs. He released the catch and wangled the points round a large coal lying in the shovel and carefully placed it on the spare fire in the grate. The old woman regarded him gravely for a moment. When he smiled back her forehead wrinkled in a taut kindly expression. Her gaze roamed upwards to the clock then her eyelids closed over.

He glanced at the clock; 8:40. He should have been home by now. The poker was lying near his foot inside the fire-surround. He wanted to rake among the ashes to see if anything red remained. Perhaps there would be enough to kindle the lump and save the fire, perhaps the new lump was too big to catch light. The rustle as he turned a page of the paper seemed to reverberate around the narrow, high-ceilinged kitchen. There was nothing to keep him. His parents would be annoyed. The bus journey home took nearly an hour and during the long winter nights they liked him to be in bed by 10 o'clock. They would guess he was here.

He got to his feet, stretched. The movement roused the old woman; she muttered vaguely about apples being in the cupboard. He drank a mouthful of water straight from the brass tap at the sink then returned to his chair.

The fire looked dead. Lifting the poker suddenly he dug right into the ashes. The old woman bent forwards and took the poker from him without comment. Gripping it with her right hand she moved her left deftly in and out the coals. Finally she balanced the new lump on smaller pieces, her thin fingers indifferent to any heat which may have remained. The poker was put back in position; handle on the floor with its sooty point projected into the air, lying angled against the fender. Wiping her fingertips on her apron she walked to the door and through to the parlour.

Neither spoke when she came back. She sat on her wooden chair and stared into the fire. Cloying black smoke drifted from the new lump. It crackled.

A little after 9:45 she looked up on hearing the light rap on the outside door. The boy stirred from his doze. He made to rise and answer but relaxed when she indicated he should remain where he was.

The outside door opened and closed, and muttering as the footsteps approached. She came in first and he followed, he appeared to be limping slightly. Mumbling incoherently and did not notice his grandson. She walked across to the sink and filled the kettle and set it on the oven gas to make a pot of tea. The boy wondered if she knew what his grandfather was saying to her. He called a greeting. The old man turned slowly and stared at him. The boy grinned but the old man turned back and resumed the muttering. His grandmother seemed not to notice anything odd about it. As the old man spoke he was scratching his head. There was no bunnet. The bunnet was not on his head.

The muttering stopped. The old man stared at the woman then at the boy. The boy looked helplessly at her but she watched the man. The expression on her face gave nothing away. Her usual face. Again the boy called a greeting but the old man turned to her and continued his muttering. The tone of his voice had altered now; it was angry. She looked away from him. When her gaze fell on him the boy tried to smile. He was aware that if he blinked, tears would appear in his eyes. He smiled at her.

Ten shillings I'm telling you, said the voice.

The boy and his grandmother looked quickly at the old man.

Ten shillings Frances, he said. The anger had gone from his voice. As if noticing the boy for the first time he looked straight at him. For several seconds he stood there, watching him, then he turned sharply back to face his wife. Ach, he grunted.

She was standing holding the apron bunched in her fists. Shaking his head the man attempted a step towards her but he fell on the floor. He sat up for a moment then fell sideways. The boy ran across crying it was okay—it was okay.

His grandmother spoke as he bent down over the old man.

He fell down, she said. He fell down.

She knelt by him on the linoleum and together they tried to raise him to his feet but it was difficult; he was heavy. The boy dragged over a chair and they managed to get him up onto it. He slumped there, his head lolling, his chin touching his chest.

He lost money, said the old woman. He said he lost money. That was what kept him. He went looking the streets for it and lost his bunnet.

It's okay Grannie, said the boy.

It kept him late, she said.

After a moment the boy asked if they should get him changed into his pyjamas and then into bed but she did not reply. He asked again, urgently.

I'll get him son, she said eventually. You can get away home now.

He looked at her in surprise.

Your mum and dad will be wondering where you've got to, she added.

It was pointless saying anything more. He could tell that by her face. Crossing to the bed in the recess he lifted his coat and slipped it on. He opened the door. When he glanced back his grandmother nodded. She was grasping her husband by the shoulders, propping him up. He could see the old man looking at her. He could see the big bald patch on the head. His grandmother nodded once more. He left then.

Even Money

It was a bit strange to see the two of them. She was wee and skinny with a really pecked-out crabbit face. He was also skinny, but shifty looking. Difficult to tell why he was shifty looking. Maybe he wasnt. Aye he was, he was fucking shifty looking and that's final. He was following her. He could easily have caught up with her and introduced hisself but he didnt, he just followed her, in steady pursuit, at a safe distance. And that is the action of a shifty character. The fact that a well-thumbed copy of the Sporting Life poked out from his coat pocket is neither here nor there. Being a betting man myself I've always resented the shady associations punters have for non-bettors. Anyhow, back to the story, the distance between the pair amounted to twenty yards, and there is an interesting point to discuss. It is this: the wee woman actually passed the man in the first place and may have seen him. She could have nodded or even spoken to him. But she did seem not to notice him. Because of that I dont know whether she knew him or not. And it is not possible to say if he knew her. He looked to be following her in an off-hand kind of fashion. When she stopped outside the post office he paused. In she went. But just as you were thinking, Aw aye, there he goes ... Naw; he didnt, he just walked on.

The Principal's Decision

The Principal here was known to have hesitated before lifting the dishcloth which he used to wipe clean the blood. I did not witness the hesitation. It was reported. When he had wiped clean the blood he glanced to where I was standing by the door. I was his associate and waited there. The body lay crumpled in its own heap. This was approved. The Principal reached towards it but only for purposes of evaluation. He was not being observed, not as such. But I saw that his eyes closed. This part of the practice is found wearisome by some. In those days I supposed that its continued existence was for decorative purposes but I took part in it. My interest was genuine. It had occurred to me that if decoration had no part in the practice then aspects of it were mere obsession. Allowing for this, if it were a form of obsession might the Principal have employed it for decorative purposes? If so I thought it admirable. I have to say that I did. At the age I then was it brought a smile to my face. It later occurred to me that he wished to be rid of it altogether, signified by the hesitation before lifting the dishcloth.

Music in the background. A nocturne by Henry Rocastle sent the Principal into a dreamy condition. Art was his passion, or so he maintained.

Would he wait until it finished? No, not him. He used his foot to manoeuvre the ruffled edge of the corpse's clothes. The untidiness made him grue. Yet his facility to operate in the most trying circumstances, withal, was here to the fore when he could never have stopped himself reaching downwards, and seemed to notice his own fingers curl in preparation. Whether he approved or not I could not say.

He had a degree of self-consciousness that I knew to respect. I watched how he sighed yet easily lifted the corpse's arm, let it fall. The arbitrary action might have made it the more natural, removing a general untidiness, so to speak. But this untidiness could not be removed from himself, not altogether. Arthritis would have him cornered in not many years hence. This was reported to me. By then I had advanced in a manner that demanded he be placed on retreat.

The Principal's very professionalism allowed the distance between truth and appearance. It is not enough to state that I respected this quality. I was experienced in the field but not expert. Whether this was enough to secure the primary position time alone would tell. I saw that the elbow of the corpse had bended. Should this have been corrected? Queries of this form can be posed objectively. Workable inferences may be ascertained by examination of the interior. A course of potential activity, from either or both, is safely predicted. Patience did not enter into these proceedings. He expected objectivity if not indifference. Either was a reward, having its own significance.

The arrangement of articles displayed on the shelving inclined towards order, irrelevant to the overall picture which was already contained in the above. Severing a limb was pointless. Such a possibility had presented itself. The result would exist as inconsistent. The Principal would not accept such. The result would further illustrate a pattern. The pattern would appear perfect, after its own fashion. Perfection of this type is not what is required. Thus the Principal looked to myself. I knew this as a ruse. I glanced at the large wall-clock. His decision belonged to an earlier generation. In these harsher times alternative courses of action were hypothetical. This was the nature of the Principality.

On another occasion, and in less immediate circumstances, I might have smiled. The next time he glimpsed the clock it would have stopped altogether. Not through any action of his. Such would never happen. He would look to me. Any decision of mine required due process. I might have smiled. My pulse had quickened and I wet my lips. The proper matter I should have happen is what would happen and what must happen, and in the correct time, but to no avail.

The Principal studied me. I knew reality and hoped that a truth lay between us. Nevertheless I departed the room. I strode into the adjacent room. I there witnessed the Principal stand alone. There would be no private smile. It was as it was and his practice dictated a practice. It was nothing to him. Personal detail is of no account in situations of this nature. Our work concerns extensions, parts and bodies. The Principal peers at the corpse, now comfortable in its presence. He could have filled a kettle, made and poured a cup of tea. Such moves enabled promotion and were victories. Their nature would enable my own promotion. It was no thanks to know that his had depended on my absence, but perhaps not.

This man for fuck sake

This man for fuck sake it was terrible seeing him walk down the edge of the pavement. If he'd wanted litter we would've given him it. The trouble is we didnt know it at the time. So all we could do was watch his progress and infer. And even under normal circumstances this is never satisfactory: it has to be readily understood the types of difficulty we laboured under. Then that rolling manoeuvre he performed while nearing the points of reference. It all looked to be going so fucking straightforward. How can you blame us? You cant, you cant fucking blame us.

Sarah Crosbie

The big house was standing empty for years before she came back. She came from America. But according to the newspaperman she had owned the house long long before. The big house stood at the end of the street, less than a hundred yards from the river. There was not much the people in the street could tell him. The old woman never spoke to them at all. She had always lived alone surrounded by cats and dogs. Sarah Crosbie. It turned out that the house had been there about two hundred years. This bit of the river had been a ford at one time. The foundations were much older than the rest of the building. Somebody called Rankine had rebuilt it and the date 1733 was discovered above a side door at the back. This Rankine was famous. The newspaperman was looking for people called Rankine to see if they were related. He thought the old woman might have been a descendant. But nobody knew. People kept away from the big house. If a neighbour or somebody ever had to go to her door she always kept them waiting on the front step. When the McDonnell Murders were going on back in the '20s a group of locals barged their way inside the big house door. They found a body behind a bricked-up chimney-piece down in the basement. A man's body, dead for many years. Nobody knew a thing about it and neither did the old woman. She had not been in the place long at the time. The police thought he might have died from natural causes and judging by the tatters of clothes he could have been a building worker or something.

When she went into hospital the newspaperman tried to gain entrance to the big house but he was refused on certain grounds. Workmen arrived the next day and they barred the place up.

It was eighteen months ago she turned up at the police office. She was in a bad state. She told them people were in her house, they had done things to her. But she would not say what things. Policemen returned to the big house with her but saw nothing suspicious. Next day a health-visitor called on her and she was admitted later on to the geriatric ward at Gartnavel Royal. A few women from the street took a bunch of flowers up to her but she just stared at the ceiling for the whole visiting hour. And it was after this the newspaperman began coming around. He goes to see her in hospital as well once or twice.

Samaritans

Heh man what d'you make of this like I mean I'm standing in the betting shop and this guy comes over. Heh john, he says, you got a smoke?

A smoke...

Aye, he says.

So okay I mean you dont like to see a cunt without a smoke. Okay, I says, here.

Ta.

Puts it in his mouth while I'm clawing myself to find a match.

Naw, he's saying, I dont like going to the begging games...

Fair enough, I says, I've been skint myself.

Aw it's no that, he says, I'm no skint.

And out comes this gold lighter man and he flicks it and that and the flame, straight away, no bother. Puffs out the smoke. I'm waiting for the bank to open at half one, he says, I've got a cheque to cash.

Good, I says, but I'm thinking well fuck you as well, that's my last fag man I mean jesus christ almighty.

the Hon

Auld Shug gits oot iv bed. Turns aff the alarm cloak. Gis straight ben the toilit. Sits doon in that oan the lavatri pan. Wee bit iv time gis by. Shug sittin ther, yonin. This Hon. Up it comes oot fri the waste pipe. Stretchis right up. Grabs him by the bolls.

Jesis christ shouts the Shug filla.

The Hon gis slack in a coupla minits. Up jumps Shug. Straight ben the kitchin hodin onti the pyjama troosirs in that jist aboot collapsin inti his cher.

Never know the minit he was sayin. Eh. Jesis christ.

Looks up at the cloak oan the mantelpiece. Eftir seven. Time he was away tae his work. Couldni move but. Shatird. Jist sits ther in the cher.

Fuck it he says Am no gon.

Coupla oors gis by. In comes the wife an that ti stick oan a kettle. Sees the auld yin sittin ther. Well past time. Day's wages oot the windi.

Goodnis sake Shug she shouts yir offi late.

Pokes him in the chist. Kneels doon oan the fler. He isni movin. Nay signs a taw. Pokes him ance mer. Still nothin bit. Then she sees he's deid. Faints. Right nix ti the Shug filla's feet. Lyin ther. The two iv them. Wan in the cher in wan in the fler. A hof oor later a chap it the door. Nay answer. Nother chap. Sound iv a key in the door. Door shuts. In comes the lassie. Eywis comes roon fir a blether wi the maw in that whin the auld yin's oot it his work. Merrit hersel. Man's a bad yin but. Cunt's never worked a day in his life. Six weans tay. Whin she sees thim ther she twigs right away.

My goad she shouts thir deid. Ma maw in ma da ir deid. She bends doon ti make sure.

O thank goad she says ma maw's jist faintit. Bit da. Da's deid. O naw. Ma da's deid, Goad love us.

The guy with the crutch

A gangrenous patch on his right leg had resulted in amputation. The people at the hospital gave him a new one which he got used to quicker than most folk in the same predicament but something happened to this new limb and now he no longer had it. For a while he moved around as best he could, making do with a walking stick of sorts; but it was not easy and he was a guy who liked travelling about the place. One morning somebody found a broken crutch and gave him it and somebody else made a cross-spar and nailed it properly down for him. This meant he was back mobile again and he used to tell folk the crutch was as adequate as anything. But eventually he stopped telling them that and soon he stopped telling them anything at all. From then on, whenever I caught sight of him, he was carrying a plastic shopper that contained most of his possessions; usually he was trudging to places over stretches of waste ground, although trudging is the wrong word because of having the crutch and so on he used to move in a rigorous and quite quick swinging motion.

The Failure

Whereas the drop appeared to recede into black nothingness I deduced each side of the chasm to taper until they merged. Each falling object would eventually land. And if footholes were to exist then discovering them could scarcely be avoided. The black of the nothingness was only so from the top: light would be perceived at the bottom, a position from where even the tiniest of specks would enable the black to be quashed. And should a problem arise, groping an ascent via the footholes would be fairly certain.

I jumped.

The sensation of the fall is indescribable.

Much later upon landing I faced black nothingness. I had been mistaken about the light. That speck was insufficient. I could distinguish nothing whatsoever. But it was impossible to concentrate for my boots were wedged into the sides and my knees were twisted unnaturally. My arms had been forced round onto my back, with my shoulders pressed forward. The entire position of my body was reminiscent of what the adept yogi may accomplish. I ached all over. Then I had become aware of how irresponsibly conceived my planning had been. It was as if somehow I had expected the bottom to be large enough to accommodate an average-sized, fully grown male.

For a lengthy period I attempted to dislodge myself but to no avail. I panicked. I clawed and clawed at the backs of my thighs in an effort to hoist up my legs until finally I was obliged to halt through sheer fatigue at the wrists and finger-joints. Sweat dripped from my every pore; and the echo consequent upon this was resounding. Beginning from the drips the noise developed into one continuous roar that increased as it rose and rose and rose before dying away out of the top. An awful realization was presenting itself to me: the more I tried and tried to dislodge my body the more firmly entrenched I would become. Think of the manner whereby a mouse seals its own fate within that most iniquitous of adhesives it has entered to search out that last scrap of food. Yes, an immediate reaction to a desperate situation may well be normal but it is rarely other than misguided. My own had resulted in a position of utter hopelessness. And the magnitude of my miscalculations seemed destined to overwhelm me. That failure to anticipate the absurdity of bottom.

No, not a mouse, nor yet a flea, could enter into that. Total nothingness. A space so minute only nothing gains entry. Not even the most supremely infinitesimal of organisms as witnessed through the finest of powerful microscopes can disturb the bottom, for here absolutely nothing exists but the point in itself, the vertex.

Acid

In this factory in the north of England acid was essential. It was contained in large vats. Gangways were laid above them. Before these gangways were made completely safe a young man fell into a vat feet first. His screams of agony were heard all over the department. Except for one old fellow the large body of men was so horrified that for a time not one of them could move. In an instant this old fellow who was also the young man's father had clambered up and along the gangway carrying a big pole. Sorry Hughie, he said. And then ducked the young man below the surface. Obviously the old fellow had had to do this because only the head and shoulders—in fact, that which had been seen above the acid was all that remained of the young man.

When I entered life was bleak.

I went to this district I used to know and it was still standing. I kept walking, wondering eventually where the hell I was and what place was I to go, and if I had a place to go how would I recognise it? By the light, by the light.

But this light was supposed to reveal to me the life. I searched for this life that I was to expect. Where was this light? I saw nothing now at all. The street was in utter darkness yet I knew about these faces too, they were at the windows, they were watching to see what choice would I make.

Fine curtains over the eyes of the folk out walking. Why had I come? It was expected. Even the air was musty, but of a certain type, as though overladen. There was a pallor.

These people thought they had a monopoly on depression. Then I arrived. This was desolate, truly desolate.

It wasnt doing me any good becoming so down, better to be angry.

I strode about and was looking for something to latch on to. I couldnt find anything. This was a danger. I had become vulnerable. So then susceptible and I could not afford that.

The sense of menace. This was no imagining. The threat was tangible. What to be done. The answer was here, here, this is where it was. I just had to find it. In finding it I would find the light, and in the light was life, so the light would guide me.

Direct Action

From the anglo saxophonics tae the northern german-
ics, the africs, the asiatics and antarctics, all whatever, I aye
get mixed up. It should all be there in black and white so
we can check wurselves out, us poor auld indo-europes, we
never know if we are coming or going. Of course we have got
nay grounds for complaint. I dont care if it is present either
in all these shit history books that get written cause it isnay
us writes them, it is them writes them, imperialism and
colonisation and all the genocides, letting these ruling aris-
tocratic ranching mafia wasp fuckers do what they like not
only to their ayn wee children but to everybody else in the
world, that is the nub. I dont blame the ruling elites because
that would be to give universality the benefit of the doubt.
I blame the underlings, not killing the rich bastards, not
wiping them out I mean to say that is inadmissible behaviour, shucking off the blame through a so-called inability to
take things into their own hands, because they never gie ye
the okay to fucking kill them, them themselves I'm talking
about, the fucking rich bastards, them gieing ye the okay
to do it, the deed.

That was what happened in other countries, the good
folk do in the evil baddy bastards unless they get stopped.
All the Yankees. Ye want to fucking giggle man know what
I'm talking about, uncontrollable. Working-class americans
I'm talking about, yous fucking mob man, still waiting for
the rulers to gie you the nod jesus christ incredible. Put us
out wur misery! Put us out wur misery! Why dont yez make
a decision for a change? an adult one, as of a mature being,

a fucking intellect, a proper intellect. Yez've been living in bad faith for a hunner and fifty fucking years. Mair.

Once ye learn that yez will have understood how come the rest of us wind up on the steps of the presidential palace, having a piss up agin the wall. That's what I'm talking about.

undeciphered tremors

In the ensuing scramble the body will melt into undeciphered tremors, undeciphered in consequence of its having been laid to rest some time prior to the call. And the "call" here must not be regarded as figurative; it will have proceeded from whence great difficulty is experienced in matters of prediction. You must also recall the state of non-well-being which exists beforehand. It is certainly the case that one has to exercise caution in hazarding a judgment but nevertheless, nevertheless, I would say if you feel the need to leap then by all means leap.

Bathroom phenomena

brushing my teeth there, I noticed these wee black things when I spat out the toothpaste residue. Looked like a couple of ants. Fuck me man what next. The girlfriend was calling on me. Shouting at me is a better way of putting it. Hurry up you!

Cannay mind if I was late or if she was wanting in. I'm just coming I shouted but I wasnay sure if I was because I wasnay sure how seriously I should take it, what had just happened. If it wasnay ants what the fuck was it? And what if it was, if it was ants. It's no a thing I wanted to share, at least no with the girlfriend. Next time she called I was still at the washhand basin, still standing there.

It was me I was looking at, seeing my lips and that wee valley thing above them, right at the nose and separating the nostrils.

These things ye never notice, yer ears poking out man, fucking weird. One of the worst was the eyes, I was feart to fucking look at them.

A Memory

O mirs! And a slice of square sausage please!

Beg pardon?

I squinted at her. A slice of square sausage—she didnt have any idea what I was rabbiting on about. A piece of absentmindedness, I had forgotten I was in fucking England. But too late now and impossible to pretend I only said "sausage" and that maybe she had misheard the first bit, something to do with "air" or "bare" maybe, "scare," "fare"—sausages are excellent fare I could have said but structured as excellent fare sausages, although the strange syntax would probably have thrown her.

Square sausage? She was frowning, but not unkindly, not hostilely, not at all, this lass of not quite tender years.

It's a delicacy of Scotland.

You what ...

It's actually a delicacy, a flat slice of sausagemeat approximately 2 inches by 3, the thickness varying between an eighth of an inch and an inch ... making the movements with both my hands to display the idea more substantially.

The girl thinking I am mad or else kidding her on in some unfathomable but essentially snobby and elitist way. It's fine, I said, just give me one of your English efforts, these long fat things you stuff full of bread and water—gaolmeat we call them back where I come from!

She was still bewildered but now slightly impatient.

Glasgow sausage manufacturers could earn themselves a fortune down here eh! Ha ha.

Yeh, she said, and walked off to the kitchen to pass in my order.

But at least she had answered when spoken to and not left me high and dry. When you think about it, imagine having to take part in such a ridiculous conversation! And yet this is how so many parties have to earn a living. One time I was aboard a public omnibus and dozing; it was a nice afternoon and the rays from the good old sun streaming in the window there. An elderly chap of some seventy or so summers sat nearby. The bus was fairly empty. The driver, a rather brusque sort of bloke I have to confess, and taking it slowly in an obvious attempt at not gaining time. At one point he stopped altogether and applied the handbrake and he sat there gazing ahead, his elbows resting on the steering wheel. Suddenly the elderly chap turns at me and he has to lean threequartersway across the damn aisle so you thought he was going to fall off his seat! He gesticulates out the window in the direction of a grocer cum newsagent shop. You see that there, he says, that shop there, he says, you see it?

Yep.

Well there used to be a cigarette machine stood there, right outside the door.

Is that right?

Aye. He nodded, giving a loud sniff of the nose, then sat back again without further ado. From the way he had performed the whole thing he was obviously a nonsmoker. But even this deduction is a boring try at producing something not so boring from something that is utterly beyond the defining pale even as a straight piece of abject boredom. If the old fellow had simply leaned over the aisle and whispered: Cigarette machines ... just starkly and in a low growling voice and left it at that, well, I would still at this very moment in my life be incredibly interested in just what precisely the full set of implications

The lass returns the lass returns!

Tea or coffee?

Tea please; and make it two thanks, one just now and one during. Mirs, the age of sauce the age of sauce!

She did not reply to that last bit though, mainly because I managed to stop myself saying it out loud thank the Lord.

Incident on a Windswept Beach

A man walked out of the sea one February morning dressed in a boilersuit & bunnet, and wearing a tartan scarf which had been tucked crosswise under each oxter to be fastened by a safety-pin at a point roughly centre of his shoulder blades; from his neck swung a pair of heavy boots whose laces were knotted together. He brought what must have been a waterproof tobacco-pouch out from a pocket, because when he had rolled a smoke he lighted the thing using a kind of Zippo (also from the pouch) and puffed upon it with an obvious relish. It was an astonishing spectacle.

Hastening over to him I exclaimed: Christ Almighty jimmy, where've you come from?

Back there, he muttered oddly and made to proceed on his path.

At least let me give you a pair of socks! I said.

But he shook his head. No ... I'm not supposed to.

The Place!

Deep water. I want to float through breakers and over breaststroking across uplifted by them. This is what I need. And upon the deep open sea. Freshwater wont do. Where are the breakers in freshwater. None. You dont fucking get them. I want to be by a sheer rockface. The steep descent to reach the sea where at hightide the caves are inaccessible by foot alone. I have to startle birds in their nests from within the caves. At hightide the rockplunge into the deep. That is what I want. That. I can swim fine and I can swim fine at my own pace and I have no illusions about my prowess. I'm not getting fucked about any longer.

There is a place I know on the coast. I cant go there. It is not in reach. The remains of a Druid cemetery close by, accounts for a few tourists. The tourists never visit the Place. Maybe they do. But it isnt a real reason for not going. There are real reasons, real reasons. My christ what a find this place was. I climbed down a dangerous part of the rockface. Right down and disregarding mostly all I know of climbing down the dangerous parts. Only perhaps 25 feet. The tide was in. I wanted to fall in. I wanted to dive in. I did not know if it was safe to dive in. If there were rocks jutting beneath the surface. So I did not want to dive in. I wanted to fall in and find out whether it was safe for diving. But if I fell onto submerged rocks I might have been killed so I did not want to fall in at all for fuck sake which is why I clung at shallow clumps of weedgrass, loose slate; and it was holding fast, supporting me, the weight. I kept getting glimpses of the caves. Impossible to reach at hightide except by swimming.

When I got down to where I could only go I saw the rocks in the depth and had to get away at that moment seeing the rocks there I had to get away at once and each grain of matter was now loosening on my touch my toes cramped and I had to cling on this loose stuff applying no none absolutely no pressure at all but just balancing there with the toes cramped in this slight crevice.

Manufactured in Paris

Whole days you spend walking about the dump looking for one and all you get's sore feet. I'm fucking sick of it. Sweaty bastarn feet. I went about without socks for a spell and the sweat was worse, streams in my shoes. Shoes! no point calling them shoes. Seen better efforts on a—christ knows what. Cant make you a pair of shoes these days. More comfort walking about in a pair of mailbags. A while ago I was passing a piece of waste ground where a few guys were kicking a ball about. On I went. We got a game going. Not a bad game. I kicked the stuffing out my shoes but. The seams split. Everybastarnthing split. Cutting back down the road with the soles flapping and that. And I had no spare pairs either by christ nothing, nothing at all. Then I found a pair of boots next to a pillarbox. This pair of boots had been Manufactured in Paris. Paris by christ. They lasted me for months too. Felt like they were mine from the start. I had been trying to pawn a suit that day. No cunt would take it. We dont take clothes these days is what they all said. Tramped all over the dump. Nothing. Not a bad suit as well. This is a funny thing about London. Glasgow—Glasgow is getting as bad right enough. They still take clothes but the price they give you's pathetic. I once spent forty-eight quid on a suit and when I took it along they offered me three for it. Three quid. Less than four months old by christ. A fine suit too. Fourteen-ounce cloth and cut to my own specifications. The trimmings. That suit had the lot. I always liked suits. Used to spend a fortune on the bastards. Foolish. I gave it all up. It was a heatwave then as well right enough but an honest decision nevertheless.

Our son is dead.

The television set had been switched on.

The perception I held of my son, now that he was dead, did seem to have changed. We were moving from the nightmare. I thought this was the case. And noted my use of the definite article: the nightmare. What did it mean? Our son was dead. He killed himself. My son did this to himself. If it was the nightmare it was ours. It was no nightmare for him. The trivial nature of this thought sickened me. People handle death in ridiculous ways. Its finality is beyond the scope of most human beings. My daughter and my other son, the sister and brother of the dead boy, were not handling this at all well. And their mother, what to say about her, of course she was not handling it, or if she was

no. The thought perishes. She was handling it. Of course she was, in her own way, it was in her own way.

Absurdity. Time and place. Meanings of life.

I came to. Where had I been?

Nothingness. There were these periods. Our brain shifts to other planets. Which planets. The thought was not mine, I moved upwards into it, moved from nothing, nothingness.

I wanted to reject life also, as he had done, and I failed to understand why this should have been impossible. My son had so chosen, used freedom and chosen freedom. But me also, surely, why not? if the child has the freedom surely the father? I am the father.

Men and women. Why between them? What is it? Parents of the same species. One to one. I was not apart from my wife. Only that I did not speak to her.

The television set had been switched on. My son's mother, now. There was the set of her shoulders. I saw the set of her shoulders, her face was turned from me. I gazed into the window and beyond the window clouds, clouds, and shapes, of faces of course, portraits. I could place my hand on her shoulder, wishing that my hand was that of my son. My wife would wish that my hand was that of my son. My wife would wish that he it was, not me.

The shoulders of women

Her son filled her head. I watched her.

Yes, the new thought, and remaining uppermost, the definite article. I desire oh I desire my desire, my desire is to

I have rejected life. I do not reject it. I have rejected it. I do not see why he could not. I can. He must have been so

Nor could it be otherwise.

Our son, say our son.

What people may say to it. People say what they say. If I should pay heed to it, I did not see why. From childhood we are not taught freedom but slavedom, taught that we are free but not that we may be free, take freedom, assert it.

We are not animals, we do not have to do what human beings tell us. My son was not under orders, and I alike. Me. Him. He was not under orders. People were telling me what might I do. But I will to not do so.

I do not enjoy free will. Free will is of me. My son chose to not exist.

Women and men may differ. Women are not like men. What are the statistics.

Tea

She was onto her feet, passing by my chair. She wanted tea. I wanted tea. She knew this. Whenever had I said no?

The door creaked and whined, requiring oil, I walked downstairs. Creaking doors are men's work, correcting the problem, we correct the problem.

I heard also the creak of the stairs. Objects are called into life. Without people it would not happen. Without people the world is dead. If we were all dead the world would be also dead, the world would no longer exist. I rose from my chair, and across to the television. I stood by it. I would not turn it on, I did not seek to turn it on. It had been switched on.

Why had I gone to there? I wished to locate the remote control. Thoughts of my son. Where was it the remote control. I smother my son. And if I did find the remote control

I was now by the window, beside my wife. My wife stared from the window. Beyond our building was the park, was a park, our park. I stood with her for many moments till then she turned, returning, to the sofa.

It was the sitting room. We had moved from downstairs.

We thought now that we had the house on our own why not transform the space, make it our space. We might do this. We would clear our son's room.

Our younger son had moved several weeks ago. Now he shared a flat with friends. He could not be with us, could not be in our home, his family home, home of us, all of us.

All children.

And what are we?

My wife was calling to me. She was calling to me. It was sandwiches. Did I hear the refrigerator door closing? Is this what I heard? Much of the time I failed to reckon with my ears. I cannot hear her from long distances, not through walls, had my hearing been a hundred percent, even then, no, no. I could not take into account matters of substance. I was required to remove to hearing range. I walked to the top of the stairs.

My son had appeared in the doorway of the bathroom. Did you want in dad? He asked did I want in. No.

I'm just going to shave, he said, the door swinging gently.

I saw it, the bathroom door, four panels. We chose it. The door shut. He shut the door. The hinges were not new.

Downstairs, the kitchen table, sandwiches and the small teapot, two cups. My wife did not look at me but to the pantry shelves. Work was to be done. We nodded to one another and I sat down, waiting for her also, she too to sit down, and the sandwiches, eating the sandwiches.

An Enquiry Concerning Human Understanding

During a time prior to this a major portion of my energy was devoted to recollection. These recollections were to be allowed to surface only for my material benefit. Each item dredged was to have been noted as the lesson learned so that never again would I find myself in the situation effected through said item. A nerve-wracking affair. And I lacked the discipline. Yet I knew all the items so well there seemed little point in dredging them up just to remember them when I in fact knew them so well already. It was desirable to take it along in calm, stately fashion; rationalizing like the reasonable being. This would have been the thing. This would have been for the experience. And I devoted real time to past acts with a view to an active future. The first major item dredged was an horse by the name of Bronze Arrow which fell at the Last in a novice hurdle race at Wincanton for Maidens at Starting. I had this thing to Eighty Quid at the remunerative odds of eleven-double-one-to-two against. Approaching the Last Bronze Arrow is steadily increasing his lead to Fifteen Lengths ... Fallen at the Last number two Bronze Arrow. This type of occurrence is most perplexing. One scarcely conceives of the ideal method of tackling such an item. But: regarding Description; the best Description of such an item is Ach, Fuck that for a Game.

A woman and two men

Some folk would think it was her keeps them the gether, without her who knows what they would do, making sure they get their grub, whatever it is, the bowl of soup, the sausage and egg, whenever she gets round to making it. But it's all an illusion, it just isnt true. It's sentimentality. It isnt a true picture at all. People just like to think that because they dont want to think something else. You see her, she hardly talks at all. And she never walks in the middle. There is something but right enough, you dont quite know what it is about her. Plus the fact she never seems to hear what the other two are talking about. She has a set look on her face all the time. Probably she knows everything they have to say anyway, their conversation's probably the same all the time. The older guy is about fifty years of age, the younger one about thirty-five, maybe even a nephew, because their relationship appears to be to do with family rather than friendship, but this is guesswork. It looks like the older one has been the longest with the woman, that the younger one just came along and decided he wanted in on the act. Unless it was a case of being invited in by the other two, or just the man, because this nephew, you dont feel he's really up to doing things for himself and neither do you get the feeling about her, about the woman, that she ever gets a say in the matter either, unless maybe she doesnt want one; she has such an inferior way of going about you can hardly imagine her ever saying much at all. But this might no be true, maybe she does, maybe she just gives the impression she doesnt. Whenever they walk down the road people stare at them, and they're open about it, because of the way they look, as if they're full of their own lives, as if what they do concerns them to the exclusion of everything else. Not only does that make them interesting it means folk feel able to stare at them without them noticing which is just as well maybe because the older guy is quite aggressive; you get the feeling about that, there's a nastiness about his face, he's always got a girn. He's definitely the chief. But then one time right enough she was on her own and she walked normal, she was swigging from a can of stout, so she might not be as docile as people think. Somebody looked at her and she looked back. The person had just came out the baker shop near the Botanic Gardens and maybe was having to step out her road—whatever, but the woman just gave her a "look." Somebody told me, apropos of what I dont know, that she "liked the men," meaning she liked to go with men. But that makes it seem she's got choices. It makes it seem like she's been able to make up her mind about things some of the time but maybe she doesnt, folk just like to think about other folk, especially women, they like to think they make up their minds about everything. But they dont, it's a fallacy.

Except I suppose there's the swing of her skirt. That lurching movement makes you think of a piece of material just thick with dirt and that is what you think of that skirt it's like you can imagine the sperm of quite a lot of men. Having said that it's important to say about her how you always think she is the one who is reflective, that it is her who reflects on what is happening roundabout; she's the one that notices what people are signifying when they look at the three of them. Plus if ever you're confronted by them, it's her eyes that stay with you; it's her you see eventually, the one who makes it hard for you. It can start you thinking about things, probably about men and women I suppose, the different types of relationships they have, how you think the women it is who carry the burden yet in such a veiled aggressive way you never feel sorry for them. They know the score. It's as if it's always them that work out the percentages. Even her, this one, the weight of her skirt, you dont for a minute think she is a hopeless victim and you dont think she is as passive as she makes out. Right enough she is a victim in the way she is just one woman having to face up to two men and you dont know quite what goes on in that situation, even if she sometimes has to find a punter if they're in trouble. That time she was overheard when they were seated on the bench down by the Kelvin, just over by the kids' swing park, and she says something that showed how she felt on her own in the company, what she said wasnt heard by the two guys—or else they didnt pay it any attention, they never "heard" her. They were on the paving stones at the edge of the flower beds, the two of them involved about something or other, or maybe nearer the point, the guy with the permanent girn on his face was talking and the nephew was listening, and then the woman says, It's no like that. Her hair straggling down her shoulders and her mouth gumsy. I think the nephew heard her and the other guy didnt because he just never expected her to speak unless spoken to, something like that. But again you know there's that way you can tell when somebody isnt very bright, maybe just how he sometimes smiles for no reason anybody can see and that nephew was a bit like that, I dont think he was the full shilling. So girny, the older guy, he turns to her: Did you speak there?

Naw.

Aye you did.

I didni.

Aye ye did.

I didni.

Ye fucking did.

Then she just shut up. Girny stared at her and you would have expected him to hit her one. I think he would've if she had said anything more. He was daring her, that's what he was doing. But she never says fuck all. She just stared at the other women, the ones with their kids playing on the swings and you wondered about that, if she was away thinking about them and relating it to herself, the way she was. It was sad. You felt as if there was this terrible awful gap between them but there wasnt really. It was all a bit weird. I just wish she could have washed her hair. I felt that for her. I felt if she had done that then the gap wouldnt have been so bad and so big, all them with their weans playing in the wee swing park, all standing there having their wee chin-wag the way women do, enjoying the sun and all that, while there was this other one, their comrade I suppose in solidarity, there she was, but they werent bothering about her, trying no to see her, then there was girny himself getting up off the bench and giving her the wire, Come on you, he said, not in actual words but just the way he jerked his thumb; the nephew as well, giving her a look, and then they went away down towards the old dummy railway.

An old story

She had been going about in this depressed state for ages so I should have known something was up. But I didnt. You dont always see what's in front of your nose. I've been sitting about the house that long. You wind up in a daze. You dont see things properly, even with the weans, the weans especially. There again but she's no a wean. No now. She's a young woman. Ach, I dont want to tell this story.

But you cant say that. Obviously the story has to get told.

Mm, aye, I know what you mean.

Fine then.

Mmm.

Okay, so about your story . . .

Aye.

It concerns a lassie, right? And she's in this depressed state, because of her boyfriend probably—eh?

I dont want to tell it.

But you've got to tell it. You've got to tell it. Unless . . . if it's no really a story at all.

Oh aye christ it's a story, dont worry about that.

Clinging On

It occurred to me I was awake. From here was difficult. I had to remind myself that the "that" was absent and its significance, its significance, the "absence" or nonexistence, or negation, and to piece together, or distinguish the several parts. In normal, or regular—I speak of the day-to-day—discourse or communication the sentence would have written as two-part comprising two clauses: "It occurred to me that I was awake." A writer of prose might well have used a "that" and therefore lost the meaning for the second clause "that I was awake" slips into a past, or simply different, time-zone. Whereas a poet might have written, or expressed the sentence separated by line-spacing, thus:

It occurred to me
I was awake.

Finer prose-writers are wary of making use of the poet's devices. They do so, but cautiously. What is clearer now is the separation between the two clauses is not just ambiguous but offers a minimum two meanings and these may be conjoined principal statements: "It occurred to me" and "I was awake." And might be expressed, or written, "It occurred to me (I was awake)." The difficulty is the use of brackets suggesting a banality which amounts not to tautology but that upon examination of one statement the other may be found. Nought can occur if one is asleep. If the act of occurrence has occurred then certainly one is awake.

Following this I can express it thus: "I was awake; this realization had taken hold of me" and, the corollary, that I might be expressed as a sentence; if so the use of the term "might" is the key to the evaporation of the space between us (me and reality). From here it follows that I may or may not be so expressed. I was aware of that. Oh God.

A Friend

She was a friend. I knew by her absence. So much that was her, the imprint she left. Hers appeared a gap in space but was a movement. By virtue of that, courses of action, how these are performed.

I learned about music. She was younger than me when she died, younger than I am now. The way I see it she did die even though technically she did not. She was not killed. Imagine "killed," a woman killed.

She was breathing beyond the accident so that she might have died. She would have smiled as she did so. She was special.

I was not present. In discussing her absence I was hearing music. This was a development. My own life, it too, it has developed.

Her absence and music there someplace, music, filling the absence.

A thought is not a finished entity if it is not one. A thought. Thoughts are more varied. Thoughts; entities in my head, inside it. So that was it too, thinking of her and her absence.

. . .

Difficulties, what we say of it, speaking of it.

And not able to get to it. I can not get to it, to her. And to her, what of her? I can not get to her, reaching to her, reaching her. It is too painful; memories, image. Neither an image; not a thought. She was a friend. Her smile was to me, hers to me.

That's where I'm at

Then there's that other case. I'm talking about the hopeless one we can all get into at some stage or another. Usually it's with a pal we've had for years, when he's pissed drunk and you're no; and you notice everybody's all staring, they're staring at the two of yous. It's when that happens the bother starts and things get quite interesting. You get the boost. It's exciting, it's the excitement, the heart starting to go and it affecting the whole body; you feel the shoulders going and if you're a smoker you're taking the wee quick puffs on the fag, sometimes no even blowing out the smoke, just taking the next yins rapid, keeping it buried deep down, letting it out in dribs and drabs, a wee tait at a time. It's because you're trying to occupy yourself. You're no wanting to seem too involved otherwise it all starts too quick; you want to calm things down, because you know what like you are. That's how as well that you can try and kid on you're no aware of what's happening. When it's a betting shop you're in you act as if you're totally engrossed in the form for the next race. If it's a pub you stare up at the telly. The broo, well ye just stare maybe at the clock or something. But all the time you're keeping that one eye peeled, watching your pal, if he's making a cunt of himself and getting folk upset. Bastards. You're just waiting, trying no to notice, trying to concentrate on other things. Fucking useless but you know it's going to happen; there's nothing you can do about it. Sometimes the waiting doesnay even last that long. You're so wound up ready to go you just burst out and fucking dig up some poor cunt who's probably no even been involved in the fucking first place! And you're at him ranting and raving:

You ya fucking snidey bastard ye what's the fucking game at all?

And he's all fucking taken aback: What d'you mean, he says.

Dont fucking give us it, you says.

But I'm no doing fuck all.

Ya lying bastard ye you're fucking on at my mate there you're fucking out of order.

What? he says.

And you start shouting: If ye fucking used your fucking eyes you'd see he was drunk ya bastard!

What! What d'you mean!! I'm just standing here having a pint minding my own business.

Minding your own business fuck all, you shout at him. And the poor cunt now can hardly speak a word cause he's bloody feart, he doesnay know what you're going to do, if you're going to fucking batter him. And he looks about the boozer for support, for somebody that knows him to defend him maybe. But nobody does. They dont actually know what happened. They never saw fuck all and dont really want to get involved. They're no really that interested anyhow, when it comes down to it, especially if it's the betting shop it's happening in because they're just waiting for the *Going Behind* call so's they can rush over and make their bets. In fact they're probably just watching what's happening to pass the time. There again but some of them will be interested, they maybe know the bloke you're digging up. They might even be the guy's mucker for all you know! But you're no caring. You dont actually give a fuck. It could even make things better. What also happens with me at a certain point is how I suddenly step out my skin and I can look down at myself standing there. Only for a split second though, then I'm back inside again and so fucking wound up I dont notice a single thing, nothing. I wouldnt even notice myself, if I was standing there and I actually was two people. One time I turned round and gubbed a polis right on the mouth. I didnt even fucking notice he was there. He tapped me on the shoulder and I just turned round and fucking belted him one, right on the fucking kisser man and he dropped, out like a light, so I just gets off my mark immediately, out the door and away like the clappers, and poor auld Fergie—that was my mate—he wound up getting huckled; and what a beating he got off the polis once they got him into the station! Poor bastard. But that's where I'm at, that kind of thing, the way it seems to happen to me. It never used to. Or did it? Maybe it did and I just didnay notice because I was young and foolish and a headstrong bastard whereas now I'm auld and grey.

Leadership

But for myself it was the greater challenge. The others might see it as theirs, as strangers to this practice. Not me. Never! They would begin, they would buckle down, draw strength from a trial shared. I admired and envied them for it.

My admiration was not misplaced though it surprised them. Of course they looked to me. I was the exemplar, the wonderful exemplar. For some I was glorious. Yes. And why? Because each manoeuvre lay within my grasp. So they presumed, failing to realize such mastery presents not liberation but a vast obligation; a world of obligation, overriding everything. Not only was my own life in thrall to the quest but the lives of those dearest to me.

Some chose not to see this, not to acknowledge the obligation. I cannot name them. Individuals are not functions. I accept this. At the same time they have roles, and enact them. At the same time they look to their own humanity; it is from here we begin.

I regret if they are hurt by such honesty.

It is true also that I smiled. I would not deny the smile. This too surprised them.

Irony is to be shared. To whom did I share the smile? To whom would the smile be shared. None. I was alone. They said I was alone and were correct, an irony in itself, but unimportant if not insignificant.

Then Later

Naybody was aboot hardly and I was hearing my ayn footsteps on the cobbles. I came out frae the back lane gon quite quickly but at the same time pacing myself. Somebody watching wouldnay know how far I had come, a couple of miles or just roon the corner. Ower my left arm was the coat, I had it folded—which didnay seem right somehow, even the way I cerried it was wrang, I knew it; but what could I dae? Maybe if I had slung it across my shooder it would have looked merr the part, but I wasnay that bothered. I crossed ower the wee path up by the canal bridge. The grass was soaking wet and there was piles of litter scattered ower the grun and further on a couple of lumps of shite beside the fence, human shite, at least that was what it looked like. Some dirty bastard. Then another pile of rubbish stacked in among the ferns—including a stack of rubbers, like a gang of weans had fun a gross and startit blawing them inti balloons.

I waited afore heading up and along the canal bank cause ye never know. And frae there ye can see a good wey away. I kept at a fast walk, needing to get out of sight quickly, there was almost nay cover at all noo, no on this side, anybody looking from the road below would have spottit me a mile away fuck, easy. When I got to the lock I had the coat bundled up and gripped in my left hon. I stooped like I was gony tie my shoelaces but I was wanting to see if the coast was clear. This is a point it can be tricky, ye can be too impatient, or else forgetful, ye think ye're hame and dry. I was doubly careful cause of it, I knew other cunts had fuckt up right at that very moment. I didnay care how long it took, within reason. I had the message oot by the tip of the handle. I let it drap and it went plopping doon inti the rushes just oot frae the bank. I couldnay resist waiting an extra second. Even daeing it I knew how stupit it was but ye know the wey it goes, that funny feeling ye're gony see it bounce back oot again, then go jumping alang behind ye, and ye dont know it's there, no till whenever, whatever—stupit—but yer heid's gon in all directions, the closer ye get the merr nervous ye ur.

So ower the lock, and that good smell; for me anywey it's a good smell, I know it's fucking detergent and aw that; but there's something aboot it. Plus cause it's sae open, ye get a breeze. Nay matter. I cerried on in the direction of the Methodist Church. This route led me oot frae between two gable-ends. I got there and then came a loud rattling noise, a lorry. I stood still. It was a delivery wagon. The driver was sterring at me. I gave him a nod but he didnay nod back. For some reason that annoyed me, it really did, fuck you ya bastard, I sterred back at the cunt. I cannay explain it, fucking idiot bastard. Nay kidding ye but the smoke was coming oot my ears. I dont know what the fuck it was to dae with. Maybe gratitude or something. I know it's stupit and there's nay reason behind it. Gratitude? I know. What can ye dae but, ye're just telling it, getting it oot. It's best getting it oot. Nay point letting it fester. Anywey, soon enough there was nothing I wantit to dae. Nothing I felt I should be daeing. Then I was walking. And I got this great feeling. It was cause I had left the driver cunt. I had met him and had the wee minor altercation, letting him see what I thought and aw that, and then when it came to the crunch I just left him stonning, I just fucking turned, no even smiling, nothing, I just fucking turned, that was that, I left him stonning, I left him to get on with it, his fucking deliveries. See if that hadnay happened, if the cunt hadnay reacted the way he had, I really dont think I would have got hame in the right frame of mind; something would have steyed unfinished.

Definitely. It sounds shite but that was the wey it was. I felt strong as fuck. Mentally as well. It was June tae and that's something, the sky was fucking great, total blue. Ye felt like gon hiking or fucking climbing; maybe if ye had a bike, take yer stove and some grub.

I watch for signs all the time. The least out the ordinary thing, ye're aye thinking this is the ane, this is the fucking ane, this is it. And see when it isnay! Hoh, jesus christ.

It doesnay matter aboot the coat. Curiosity killed the cat. So they say anywey.

this was different

talking about the weariness, the feeling of fatigue, having to raise yourself off the chair, up off the chair, fighting to raise yourself, and if you manage it, to get yourself up from the chair and are still feeling bad then okay, just go to bed, go upstairs and lie down; switch on the radio, and next on from there—whatever, whatever you need, it is a need, the recognition

but I could not manage it. My eyelids closed and I sighed: a weary irritation, self-irritated, oneself, untrusting in oneself: was I really too bad to rise from the damn chair? or was I pretending, did I have a few gasps before the last, the penultimate

Does it matter, if beyond it, was I beyond it, I was beyond it.

Music, okay, trying that. I thought I was incapable but ahead lay the barrier and through it I would go, I would to go, I willed such.

Later I thought I heard the outside door, someone there and knocking loudly and this was so beautiful; in the act itself, beauty in the act. I would rise, indeed required to rise, seeing who was there

but no, I was incapable, I lay back on the chair. The knocking ended. Whoever, whomso, might it have been, could it have been, whomso

friends, and had family, whoever was there. I wondered and to worry, would to have worried.

the tired tired, of tiredness, acutely so. It was acutely so. I could only lie, on the chair, the back on the chair, armchair, a comfortable armchair, the great comfort of it.

When had I experienced this before? It was an acute weariness, an acute weary ness, I

if someone had known, if it was known, I was here.

When Annie was with me

It was fine for her, she fell asleep. She did this in the middle of a conversation. I was flummoxed. Then too the word "body" as she used the word: or the word cropping up as between she and I, she and he, the "s" nuzzling the "he," "body," I was thinking "bawdy" and writing "bawdy." It was that period in our relationship when all she had to do, only the one thing, whatever that might be, thus that the gist, lost forever, so I cuddled her immediately, I always did, and hardons, Annie.

People can disbelieve me if they wish. It was the same where we lived in that old part of the city. I drank in a restaurant whose management hated the sight of us. When asked the nature of my employment, as they put it, how I earned my living, and I told them they smiled sarcastically. When I added, It's true! I would see Annie wince. And so I stopped doing it.

By then she had moved in with me. We were heading to the west coast, we hitched a lift on the outskirts of a village named in the old language, and translated by the locals as "Cadaver" which I thought interesting and wanted to use. At the same time we were glad to pass through swiftly. I said we should return, the place had a feel to it that I thought creative and I thought lyrics might have been easier to work from within.

Except then, when winter came so too the horrors of such wind, oh the wind, in this part of this country, downpours, the downpouring, freezing rain. Annie was just like Oh God surely it will stop, and was she referring to me rather than any natural element. That made me smile, and became a verse.

But it was not true. I knew I was hearing things, her body on mine, until that moment, not until that moment. We were in a licensed so-called restaurant for a few drinks, it being well in among the wee hours, after hours. It cost someone a fortune. Was this laid on by the organizers? Who knows. She was not acquainted with them, none of them, the folk surrounding, none. And I knew nothing, who I was, nothing, I was just nothing, nothing. I was nothing.

So I was in favour, if she was in favour.

It would be boring as hell but we had thirsts to quench, hunger to appease, time to kill. It was me they were watching, and they kept on with it. I did not grudge them the watching. How could I? It would pass. It did pass. Just let them keep out my road, I whispered.

Annie winked, nearly. She said that she had not winked, if so it was unintentional; a wink more a blink. I found this hard to believe but accepted it, that I should not lay such heavy significance on a minor example of "life instances" which was her name for this phenomenon. She called it an example of a life instance.

I was always smiling when I was with her. There was that thing always, she just made me smile, no matter how tough the moment, being trapped in here and out in there. The rescue arrived. How come! Somehow it did, it always did. That was Annie; that was the great thing.

The Witness

As expected the windows were draped over with offwhite curtains, the body dressed in the navyblue three-piece suit, with the grey tweed bunnet on the head. Drawing a chair close in I sat smoking. I noticed the eyelids parting. The eyes were grey and white with red veins. The cigarette fell from my fingers. I reached quickly to get it up off the carpet. A movement on the bed. Scuffling noises. The head had turned. The eyes peering towards me. There was not a thing I could say. He was attempting to sit up now. He sat up. I placed a hand of mine on his right forearm. I was trying to restrain him. He wanted to rise. I withdrew my hand and he swivelled until his feet contacted space. I moved back. His feet lowered to the carpet then the rest of his body was up from the bed. He stood erect, the shoulders pushed back. The shoes on his feet; the laces were knotted far too tightly. I picked the grey tweed bunnet up from where it now was lying by the pillow and passed it to him, indicating his head. He took it and pulled it on, smoothed down the old hair at the sides of his head. I was wanting to know if he was going to the kitchen: he nodded. Although he walked normally to the door he fumbled on the handle. He was irritated by this clumsiness. He made way for me. I could open the door easily. He had to brush past me. The cuff of his right sleeve touched my hand. I watched him. When he got to the kitchen door he did not hesitate and he did not fumble with its handle. The door swung behind him. I heard his voice cry out. He was making for her. I gazed through the narrow gap in the doorway. He was struggling with her. He began to strike her about the shoulders, beating her down onto her knees; and she cried, cried softly. This was it. This was the thing. I held my head in both hands.

Human Resources Tract 2: Our Hope in Playing the Rules

The Crime has Occurred.

A crime is a criminal act. We should not have committed the act. If we had not committed the act the crime would not have occurred. We did it. Thus we committed the crime. We cannot "take it back" as some will suggest. Colleagues think it possible, it is not possible. Actions cannot be undone. We can regret the performance of such an action if it is we who performed such. The deed, however, is done and none travels back in time. We might wish to withdraw the action but that is impossible. Actions may not be withdrawn.

Of our guilt none may know. Not in this world. This is a remarkable feature. We should pause and take proper cognisance of it. Some will ponder the causal relationship. Might we have effected the end result? At all costs it will be known that no consequence shall be suffered. The action we have performed will be known by others. It may or may not be considered a "crime." Whether or not the action accords to the term "crime" is a judgment in itself and outwith our scope. Should this prove the case it will be recognised as our decision, acknowledged as our decision, respected as our decision.

Others will not judge for us. This will not happen unless so allowed. Whether or not people agree with us is of a certain significance but without bearing, unless so allowed.

We may believe ourselves guilty of having committed an action that we should not have committed. We know that in the judgment of other people our action was no crime. But this is not enough for us. We know that we committed a wrongful action and further may believe ourselves guilty of a crime (see para 1). Our quest begins from there and will reveal inconsistencies. Nothing is more certain. In petty detail truths are revealed. Our more risible judgments will have derived from sentimental generalizations.

If we remain in guilt we cannot be with God and may not enter His province. The process of absolution begins with our acknowledgement of guilt. We confess our guilt. It is only through this confession of guilt that our guilt becomes known. In order that we may be absolved our guilt must be known. We confess our guilt to God. This is achieved through direct communication by prayer and other spiritual methods. The magnitude of God's greatness is forever beyond our ken and cannot be a concern.

In many religions there are human mediators who assist us in our quest for absolution. If we are uncertain how to go about matters then the mediators will advise and guide us. A list of those is readily available. They are thought more knowledgeable than ourselves. They are to have received training in the ways and means that direct communication with God may be obtained. The ultimate end is the ultimate mystery. Mediators are taught this most difficult of roles; that which appears to approximate to "an acquisition of the will to win the attention of God."

Confessing the crime in theological terms is an important solution and we should not hesitate to embrace such. Our preference is towards these religions into which most of us are born, that place humankind close to the heart of the universe. The heart of the universe is God and His is a beating heart. The centre of the universe is the province of God. God is primary and ultimate dispenser of justice. This alone is our foundation.

Yes we committed the crime. Our examiners may be notified.

John Devine

My name is John Devine and I now discover that for the past while I've been going off my head. I mean that the realization has finally hit me. Before then I sort of thought about it every so often but not in a concrete sense. It was actually getting to the stage where I was joking about it with friends! It's alright I would say on committing some almighty clanger, I'm going off my head.

On umpteen occasions it has happened with my wife. Two nights ago for instance; I'm standing washing the dishes and I drops this big plate that gets used for serving cakes, I drops it onto the floor. It was no careless act. Not really. I had been preoccupied right enough and the thought was to do with the plate and in some way starting to look upon it not as a piece of crockery but as something to be taken care of. This is no metaphor; it hasnt got anything to do with parental responsibility. My wife heard the smash and she came ben to see what was up. Sorry, I said, I'm just going off my head. And I smiled.

Out There

I had to do something new. My way of operating was not so old yet I seemed to have forgotten how to do anything else. I didnay like that. My eyes kept closing too. I was not requiring to sleep, not thinking about sleep at all. Although it was in sleep the thoughts came. I didnay want these thoughts but I got them. And I could not care less if I was caught in the act. I had given up worrying about this months ago, several months ago, last year at least.

Mental preoccupations, I couldnay afford them either. Waves of sleep but I would not allow them to engulf me. Waves of sleep.

I looked for my diary.

It was around somewhere, roundabout—where? Reflections.

My diary, reflections. Also the usual aches; how come these aches all round my right ear itching and fiddling footering scratching and oh jesus the back side of the head; right side, and just aching, oh fuck. Finding myself in the same old situation was less than helpful. I needed something new and to hell with it.

But in a new form? No, I didnay think so. I didnt think at all, I didnt, just that, no, not such that I couldnay handle it, and readily, reserving my energy for the strug-gle itself, not the conditions towards it, setting them for what lay ahead, that was the danger, constant temptation similar to giving up, the concession to it oh god I could no longer just be here, and just being here.

Although I would be walking into the new place soon. I would be arriving there. So I would keep on. I would. This is not proper decision-making, only a function, continuing as a person.

I knew more was demanded. So what? I knew myself inside out. To be upright, the one deep breath, opening the eyelids to greeting the day. Extant, that was what I looked for, having become, become it: extanticity.

But the temptation oh god and to make it as a question: Why do my eyes close? No, I do not believe it; I do not accept it. All the time they were closing. So what? That is nothing, that is bloody nothing.

I wasnay supposed to sleep. I knew that I could, if I lay down and the scene had been set but how, how, colder, to sleep.

I didnt want even to be doing that, and if it was cold— colder, okay, then my eyes

Half an hour before he died

About half an hour before he died Mr Miller woke up, aware that he might start seeing things from out the different shapes in the bedroom, especially all these clothes hanging on the pegs on the door, their suddenly being transformed into ghastly kinds of bodies, perhaps hovering in mid air. It was not a good feeling; and having reflected on it for quite a few minutes he began dragging himself up onto his elbows to peer about the place. And his wrists felt really strange, as if they were bloodless or something, bereft of blood maybe, no blood at all to course through the veins. For a wee while he became convinced he was losing his sanity altogether, but no, it was not that, not that precisely; what it was, he saw another possibility, and it was to do with crossing the edge into a sort of madness he had to describe as "proper"—a proper madness. And as soon as he recognised the distinction he began to feel better, definitely. Then came the crashing of a big lorry, articulated by the sound of it. Yes, it always had been a liability this, living right on top of such a busy bloody road. He was resting on his elbows still, considering all of it, how it had been so noisy, at all hours of the day and night. Terrible. He felt like shouting on the wife to come ben so's he could tell her about it, about how he felt about it, but he was feeling far too tired and he had to lie back down.

A Drive to the Highlands

Space was necessary. Not as always but there and then. I come from a large family and space is the one unmistakable entity, people might say, necessary entity. Yes but not for this. I could think of the Highlands and those empty places, empty mountains and hills and the entire area roundabout the lochside. I was not used to it and would have given my eye-teeth to become used to it. But at that precise moment I needed gone from here and there, there was the place. Nothing to do with anything except that. But was it possible?

All morning I thought about it. By the time I was having the pre-work shower I still was thinking about it, I could not escape the fantasy, and since now a thought it was do-able, ergo.

I had a pal, Carl. He had a car. I texted him. Fancy a drive?

Yeah man fifteen.

Quarter of an hour. That was the brilliant thing with Carl, he didnt bother about stuff hardly at all. If ye asked him to do something it was aye or naw, aye if he could, naw if he couldnay. I walked round to his place. I saw he was inside the car already. Fancy a drive up the Highlands?

Okay.

How come you didnt come round and get me? I said.

He nodded his head. He understood the question but didnt have an answer.

Anyway, I said, I liked the walk. I wasnay sure if ye were working today. Good you werent.

I was working, supposed to be.

Me too. Hell with it, just to think and breathe air, real air, breathing real air, air from the deep lochs and wind, wind. In the city you dont get it, not a real wind erupting from the depths of these inland lochs where the water gushes from the depth of the earth rather than the oceans and the ice-floes breaking around the Arctic. Are ye listening?

Carl nodded slightly, staring out the window. By now we were on the road. He hardly spoke at all, especially driving. If he was thinking at all, in opposition to me or not. He never showed it. No matter. Just that face; the concentration. But was it? Maybe it wasnay. Maybe he wasnay thinking anything at all, never mind original, an original thought. Ye never knew with Carl. With me but I was full of thoughts and ideas and all sorts that never came to nothing, Nothing. Never. Who cares. I didnay and neither did Carl. He just joined in. Whatever plans. Anything and everything. All kinds. Not so much plans even just like, just like whatever. I was never a guy that plans. Never ever. What is the opposite of plans. I didnt have plans. Except weird sort of thoughts and ideas and kind of weird, immediacy, immediate, immediate moves, moves to make right at this moment in this here and now. Imagine a hitchhiker, I said, and she had a pal. Two girls, from Switzerland or someplace. Imagine that and they wanted a hitch with us, they just like . . .

Carl smiled.

You maybe know why I said Switzerland but I have this notion resembling a why, just these good fun girls who dont need future plans. What job do you work at and where do you stay, college or university: fuck all that. So they want to know about you instead of just relaxing, just relax, enjoy the drive, a glass of wine or something, have a smoke, listen to the music. The girls I know cant listen, never ever man ye put on music and sit back but they dont. One minute just, they dont, and they're talking, aye talking, asking a question or whatever, telling ye something, that's what they do. The thing is too, I said, going with the Arctic, why not the Antarctic? How come? I'm thinking about penguins except you dont get penguins, not in the Highlands.

Carl nodded, then frowning. Yeah, he said.

I sat back, seeing out the window.

Margaret's away somewhere

Of course Margaret wasnt the sort of woman you trusted. She had that way of looking at you as if she was wondering how she was going to con you this time and if she could just take it for granted she would get away with it or else did she have to work out methods of escape afterwards. It put you on your guard. And I mean everybody, even the paperboy or the milkboy, when they came to collect the money at the end of the week, they were wary as well. You couldnt help watching her. Even if you were talking to somebody else, if you were standing somewhere where she was, if you were talking to somebody, in the post office for instance, you were always watching her at the same time, so that your eyes might meet and she could go surprised, a bit taken aback, as if she was having to think to herself "Did he see me there?" but then she would give a wee self-possessed smile and you would give her one back. It was funny the way she managed it, because the truth is she would have won as far as that particular exchange is concerned. And if ever she had to actually say something it would nearly always be a "What was that?" and this made you know she hadnt been listening to a word you said, this because she rated you so low there was nothing at all you could say would ever interest her, whereas probably you thought she had been waiting for you to speak to her all the time. It wasnt easy being in her company and you were always glad to see the back of her, I mean relieved. But it didnt dawn on me she had disappeared till a long time after—I mean when you told me about it, about how she hadnt been around for a while, it hadnt dawned on me.

A Family Meeting

Blood is alright, I said, shite is the problem. Or should I say shit?

I dont care what you say it's a horrible word, said my young sister—my big sister was there too. So was my brother, he was scowling at me.

Sorry but I had to say it.

No ye didn't, she said.

In your opinion, I said. It all depends on the family. That is the trouble. In some families the veins get clogged with shite—excrement if ye will—and this is what I wanted to discuss with you this morning. Nay point looking at me like I smell.

Yes, said my young sister, you always have to do something dont you?

I grinned.

My brother had tried a smile. Me grinning stopped him in the act. He was looking at me but. I was not looking at him and he was very aware of this. He thought I was trying to put one over on him. We arent worth a candle, said he. Is that what you're telling us?

If ue want to be told. Yes, I am.

Then to hell with you and your problems.

I smirked.

Yes, and yer sarcasm.

Oh well. I shrugged.

I forgot to mention the in-laws. They were there too. Plus a mother and a father who were not present. This family meeting was supposed to be about them. I was trying to get the discussion going. I had been trying for many a month. Years in fact. It seems like years anyway, I said, I would be as well talking to that effin television screen.

Well, if you would stop your swearing, said my young sister.

I chuckled.

Oh the cheek of you! she cried.

My brother was frowning, not knowing if there was something else he could be doing. This frown was him buying time. I managed not to laugh.

My big sister sighed. This is not taking us anywhere.

I agree, but that's this family. Family is family is family. That creates a problem in itself. I've been grappling with it for years. It's now beyond me. It's okay for you, I said, you live in England, you dont have to deal with it. I do, because if I dont who else will?

You are so arrogant, said my young sister.

One of the weans had a headset on: thump thump thump, interrupting the progression not just of my thought but collectively, everybody in the damn room. We were all affected: thump thump thump. It was almost funny. A nephew. A cheeky wee bastard. They said he was independent but it was mair than that. And this thump thump thump was mair than that. His father who was my brother-in-law had made it an issue from earlier days, how if one of our children should be into his or her own world in such a way that it impinged on the sanity of other folk then it was up to them to check their behaviour and they had that right which was not a privilege, it was a right. That was my thinking too.

Nowadays it was wishful.

That was one thing. It was neither a right nor my place to grab the wee bugger by the throat and strangle him but I would to have. That was the right, just to tell him aff. My sister, her son. Who was I to interfere. Her big brother but so what? That was their thinking.

Yes well it was not mine. Not when it drove one fucking bananas. Others could complain to each other. I had nobody. My wife could not bear my family. She could not stomach them. Off she went to see a pal for the day, leaving me to weather the storm. Thus I was alone amongst them.

Where was she anyway? She was never here when I needed her. And I needed her now. She was always herself. That was the trouble. She was never a member of the family. Not this one. She always was herself. It always amused me about her. I chuckled.

You're so smart, muttered my young sister.

Sorry, I said, thinking about how now and again she allowed members of this family to creep closer to her—creep being the operative term, although so what, that was family, we are all family and we all creep about, our family, yours mine and whoever's, even her, if it was hers and not mine, and I was sick of it. That is how come I asked for a meeting, I was sick of it, just so sick of it.

This was a general malaise, unaccountable, and no prescription, no medicine never mind medication, I could have done with a drink and to hell with it. To hell with this, I would have said, would have loved to have said, and got up and left, except it was me called the damn meeting.

The Small Bird and the Young Person

—as for example were a Small Bird to thud into your face.
Consider the following: a Young Person is chancing to stroll
upon an island somewhere in the Firth of Clyde. THUD. A
Small Bird crashes onto the bridge of the nose of the Young
Person. The day has been fine, a mid-afternoon with an
Autumnal sun warm enough to enable the coat to be discarded should the breeze die. Now, the idea of ducking to
avoid the collision will never have occurred to the Young
Person for quite often you will come to find that birds do
fly on courses indicative of just such a collision. At the last
possible moment, however, they will dip a wing sufficiently
to swerve off. Not this time! While the Young Person is
staggering the Small Bird will drop to the ground and lie
still, its feathers stiffly spread. Having covered face with
hands the Young Person will, in time, withdraw the hands
for an examination of the person. But effects to the body
will almost certainly be minimal; a little blood, the slight
cut, a possible temporary swelling. And nothing else, apart
from the stunned Bird. While the view hereabouts will be
extensive the Young Person can see nobody in sight. After
a moment the spread feathers begin fluttering; soon the
Small Bird starts rising in helicoptereal fashion. Staring at
it with furrowed brow the Young Person will turn suddenly
and yell, before dashing headlong in the direction of the
shingle shoreline.

A woman I can speak about

There is a neighbour and I could not speak about her. If I did speak of her what would people say? I think I would be blamed. At the particular time I did not, and would not.

It is terrible and ruthless male practice to speak badly of any woman, old as well as young. I cannot abide males engaging in this, even to hear about it from others. I wish they would say it when I was not in the company, if they have to say it at all. It is such crap.

But I was there when it happened, the better to describe it as factual, so that is that. Yes I can speak of her now. Let me say that we should not shy away from the terrible truth that not only males addressed her in demeaning terms, females did likewise. Their terms were so much worse, so much more demeaning. I thought they were her friends. Supposedly, they were.

They were disgusting. Friends like that are disgusting. Among them were people she would have trusted. Had I been her, well, it is easy to say one thing rather than another.

She was pretty too. All people are, in their own individual way. They say beauty is skin-deep. Especially those who are not. But she was pretty and males would have wanted her. It was not this disgusted me. I doubt even that I was disgusted. We use words as we do, but not always precisely. It was a natural feeling and even a mother puts up with that, otherwise it is breakdown, or suicide.

The inhumanity of it that when it had gone she left no recollection, there was no recollection; nothing lingered. Women vanish from memory. What about these men? I wondered about them. Had they any morality at all. My own mind presents its own anomalies, unique to itself. At crucial intervals I also have no memory. Please God let me not speak of that. Other people thought I was her friend but I was not. It was not through friendship I spoke on her behalf. Here can be misunderstandings but I do not believe this to have been one. I say that now and forever will say it, please God.

A Hard Man

The best thing he did was commit suicide. Before he did he apologized, but no one was sure for what. Some thought the act itself, others past misdemeanours. I was not convinced. When I heard he had done it I thought "kill the bastard," but to whom was I talking? And so what if he was already dead, just what exactly did I mean?

Did it mean anything? Did it matter if it didnay?

Okay not at all, okay, who gives a fuck, okay.

Anyway, it wasnay me asking these questions. I had long ago ceased talking to myself. Way way back. Stultifying fucking monologues man they drive ye fucking nuts, truth be told.

I hardly knew the bastard. Talking personally. I thought I did. I didnay. I knew I didnay like him but so what. It was respect man I had nay respect for him. Nayn at all.

So what?

Nothing. There isnay anything. Fuck all. So he was a hard man, so what? So if I should care, or if it makes a difference. Does it fuck man suicide is suicide, I dont give a fuck who it is.

The Appearance of Absence

People have "vantage points." This was his. He was entitled to his; as entitled to his as anyone. He was not good at games but had the right to play them. He was not, for example, as good as them, but what difference does that make. It was not his problem. They had theirs he had his. His game interested him. Theirs did not. It concerned a particular psychosis. He was no snivelling coward and had no wish to become one. Nor was he unique. Of course not. All the same, he was singular. Everybody is. He was one of everybody. That is the way he liked it.

There is a fall to that expression, a lilting note or downward loop, giving the statement the ring of truth. The rise is the wakening period; the fall is the return to non-consciousness. He was not obsessive but if there is a truth then seek it out. He may have been a stickler. Games of that nature relate to masquerade. One thinks of a story by E A Poe. He read it in his teens. Poe is an author for youth. So many authors are to be read in one's youth. In the story by Poe the limits are set to one's own existence and youth requires to learn that limits exist.

He saw his life as a masquerade. Day upon day we perform a series of rituals. The set of these rituals is the individual, in singularity. This series exists for each twenty-four-hour period and every individual lives within his and her own series. It is indefinite and the sum of these is the unique being. Upon this personal level death was preferable to life.

This was the realization. It had become so for him, inevitably. Others might have life, he desired not so much death as absence: almost absence, having that appearance. He felt this so strongly while walking, and walking by the sea, and by the roar, that lifting and rising, the fall, and other individuals, he saw them walking so slowly, dragging their heels and lingering stares to the horizon as to the world, the far off voyage, their dogs, dogs on the leash, the dogs also, mournful.

That place where now he dwelled was a dreaming world. There is a strangeity, a wistful factor; perhaps a presence: Ballantrae. Stevenson and Poe. This was Ayrshire, for some a mundanity. Adults enter, linger. A place of uncles and aunties. His parents separated when he was young. His Uncle and Aunt had given him a home. Each school term this was the refuge, this was the end of term, if only he could reach end of term. They did this for his good, offering stability at this most difficult period. That his parents might have surmounted their differences and resumed living together. They did not. He could not forgive them. Could anyone?

He was relieved to stay with his Uncle and Aunt. Both were readers, his Uncle especially. It was a vast pleasure to trawl their bookshelves. When the adults learned of his interest they enjoyed talking to him, to the amusement of both.

He and his Aunt wheeled his Uncle around in his wheel-chair. She was in her late fifties; it was laborious. The boy was twelve, soon to be thirteen. Theirs was a love-match. Even he could see this. They had two children of their own: each lived in foreign parts, each had families of their own.

Here too is where he discovered "love-benches," these seats where the names of the dearly departed are localised, those who walked these paths and rested, required to rest, and generalized how it was down through the generations and so, as entering the later years, around this part of Ayrshire, for each bench had stories, many stories, some dark, mysterious trysts, unknown lives, secret desires. True desires were never yearnings. He had yearnings, a yearning. He would not describe it as such until older, and discovered that oblivion was not the state he sought, but rather the state of being almost. Where is he? He is not here. He is almost here. Where is he? Must he be some other place?

It was a game with an end and the end was absence. The game itself did not end. He dropped from it, or became so dropped. His participation at an end. He continued to read stories; a pastime rather than endeavour. The distinction casts light, offers illumination. Success might provide commentary on one's own life, one's entire life. In his teens he thought to stand or fall by the reading of certain individuals whose names he preferred to conceal. Suffice to say they were German, if Russian Germans in thought and practice. His suspicions were aroused. They seemed altogether untroubled. Life came too easily, too easily. And on what grounds, he could not say, nor yet conceive, not of these grounds. What were these grounds? People have need of their own. Needs are human. If they cannot obtain such they cannot continue. People are entitled to that. All of us. We have those as a need, and the need is a right, and he would have that right, this was an entitlement, asserted and taken.

ONE SUCH PREPARATION

THE INITIAL REBELLIOUS BEARING IS AN EFFECT OF THE UNIFORM'S IRRITATION OF WHICH AMPLE EVIDENCE IS ALREADY TO HAND. BUT THIS KNOWLEDGE MAY BE OFFSET BY THE POSSIBILITY OF BEING TOUCHED BY GLORY. AT THE STAGE WHERE THE INCLINE BECOMES STEEPER THE ONE IN QUESTION STARED STEADFASTLY TO THE FRONT. HIS BREATHING, HARSH AS BEFITS AN UNDERGOING OF THE EXTREME, NEVER BETRAYED THE LEAST HINT OF INTERIOR MONOLOGUE. THERE WAS NO SIGN OF A WISH TO PAUSE AND NOR WAS THERE ANY TO REDUCE OR TO INCREASE PACE. HIS CONTROL WAS APPROPRIATE. THE AIR OF RESIGNATION GOVERNING HIS MOVEMENT CONTAINED NO GUILT WHICH INDICATED AN AWARENESS OF OUTSIDE INFERENCE. IT WAS AT THIS PRECISE MARK THE SATISFACTION EMERGED IN THE PROCEEDINGS. HIS ARMS AROSE STIFFLY UNTIL THE FINGERTIPS WERE PARALLEL TO THE WAISTBAND. HIS GAZE HAD BEEN DIRECTED BELOW BUT HE CONTINUED STARING TO THE FRONT AS IF EXPECTING OR EXPERIENCING A REACTION. WHAT WAS THE NATURAL SUMMIT MIGHT WELL HAVE BEEN INTERPRETED AS OTHERWISE.

Calm down son

Bastard, what was fucking keeping her, this was just a nightmare.

It was me, what happened to me. At college too, where I met her, that was where I met her, I was the harum-scarum student, fucking eedjit, the one who cheeked the dons, the fucking dons man know what I'm talking about, I cheeked them. She perceived alternatives, alternatives, as far as I was concerned, too many, too many. Honest. Fuck. Even now, even now

jesus christ

Mind you, totally dependable, as women go—lasses, as they go, ye just christ almighty go back the way, ye go back the way, ye just like eh

That is it with me, that is me. What happened.

jesus christ,

I'm

nevertheless

it's jumpy, ye get jumpy. That's lasses, lasses are lasses.

It isnay that but it's mair than that, mair than that, just like what happened, what happened, lasses, lasses are lasses—so what lasses are lasses, so what?

Harum scarum. What is that tae I mean college, jesus christ.

She knew. I didnay. Round towers and grass lawns; all that kind of shite, boaters, what's boaters? A fucking boater jesus christ, fucking time man where was she. It isnay enough, one does not go on that way, one doesnt, ye just fucking dont man ye just fucking oh god ye just

because ye dont know, no with her. I dont, never, I
never
    I was lost with her, without her, just lost and ye are
just standing there and
    christ knows. Even at college, I never knew, seeing
them all, that class thing, class, phantasmagoria, boaters
down the river, white dresses and flouncy petticoats, wee
umbrellas, in the shirt sleeves, harum scarum in the skiff
punting like fuck; oh here she comes; who is she walking
to? To whom. Me. Me, walking to me, jesus christ
    jesus christ, ye're just fucking
    that's what I'm talking about, just like

Fr Fitzmichael

Outwith the Palace Grounds the sudden reversals were being met by widely differing though often violent retorts. But the worthy Fr Fitzmichael continued to perform his duties in a no less perfunctory manner: at 3:24 a.m. he was awake and set for his first of the day; the second was followed by the third and the fourth. When that time for the sixth had arrived he was to be seen sheltering beneath the large tree near to the Boundary. November is a dismal month. A month of the Spirit. A dismal month requires Spirit. In order that we may progress into the next, more than usual attention is to be given over to entities whose design is Spiritual. Fr Fitzmichael then stretched his arms, he was reclining with his back against the gnarled trunk of the tree; a trio of ants had appeared on the tips of his toes. With a smile he leaned to cuff at them with a flick of his over-garment. Such things are we brought to. The condition being a Triumvirate of Hymenopterous Insects on the tips of one's toes. Hello. His call to a passing Brother was greeted with an astonished raising of the eyebrows. He waved. November. A month of the Spirit. Spirit and Dismality are equidistant. The Brother hurried off in the direction of the Palace. So, it would seem the Game is to be up. Fr Fitzmichael's smile was benign. The attention of the Superiors shall be brought to bear heavily. So it must be. The tree contains ants. One enters the Palace Library to peruse the books of one's pleasure. One enters the Palace Grounds to be confronted by unimaginable entities whence pleasure is to be derived in the month of the Spirit. Take an acorn. Place it in the palm of one's hand. Squeeze.

On Leave

Daniel noticed the baby looking, twisting about on Michaela's lap. But it was looking past him. He followed the look. An old guy on the seat across the aisle making faces. The baby was looking at him. The old guy was smiling. The baby looked like whatever it was, what it was doing in its own face. It just seemed to be looking, trying to figure out the old man, what he was doing. Daniel didn't know either. He had been thumbing the magazine, the adverts; mainly it was adverts. He raised the bottle of water and swallowed a mouthful, returned it into the net compartment on the back of the seat in front.

The old man looking again, it was Daniel he was looking at. Right at him. Daniel didn't react. He turned a page of the magazine. The old guy stopped looking now.

Sometimes his mother did the same, she just looked, seeing things, not meaning anything, not being critical. He hadnt seen her for a while. Probably she was okay. People did that, they looked; that was what they did. The baby, its head lolled, drooping, staring down, he was awake, just staring. What at—the floor. Its head nodded, maybe going to sleep.

A wee bit later and Michaela was holding it up, she was arranging the clothes, to do with that. She saw Daniel and smiled. Daniel nodded. She was doing it now with one hand, holding up the baby, doing the clothes with the other. She managed it easy.

The baby too, looking over her shoulder, the row behind, just looking at something, whatever it was. Daniel shifted slightly to see back over the seats. It was a woman in the row behind who was making faces and smiling then talking: Oh oh oh oh see you see you oh you're a good boy, oh oh oh. The baby was staring at her. His name was Daniel too. Michaela wanted to call him that. Daniel didnt, not really, he didnay really care.

She was finished what she was doing with the clothes, lowered the baby down on to her lap, so it was facing into the back of seats in the row to the front, and its head lolled.

Its wee head. It was sleeping. Maybe its head would get sore.

Daniel reached in to the net compartment, brought out the magazine, thumbed through it again. The watches were good, they were good deals. But he didnay need one. He yawned and shut the magazine, returned it to the net compartment. There was a change in the sound of the plane engine. Michaela gestured to him. Quarter of an hour to landing. Och well. She smiled. Daniel nodded, raising his eyebrows. She was looking past him. That old guy again; nosy old cunt. He was looking at Daniel and smiling. What about? Was he to smile back? Old folk. How come he was smiling? The baby, it was the baby. He was seeing the baby, looking at the baby and the baby was looking at him. That old face. What age was he? You never know with people. Some are old and look young. He winked, the old guy. Its head twitched and a look on its face, his cheeks, the wee boy, and his eyes too, just staring now, staring at the old guy and like he was going to smile then not, then not, his head nodding, looking down: a twitch in his neck, whatever that was, what that was: his neck? Daniel frowned. He nudged Michaela and she gestured, meaning what, he shrugged. The baby, he said.

Here. She smiled and passed him it.

Daniel moved, raised his hands to take it and she gave him it. He with one hand underneath, the other on the shoulder then the other shoulder, so both shoulders. It squirmed, squirming, the baby was squirming but he just held it, he didnt press. He removed his right hand, put it to the side, to the baby's hip, to the waist, its clothes were tight, just tight or the nappy or maybe, whatever, something, just tight, too tight maybe. That whimpering sound, oh God, that whimpering sound. Daniel's eyes blinked. He hated it, babies doing that, he hated it. This whimpering sound it was like crying, it was worse than crying. Daniel held him up, holding him under the shoulders, the armpits. He was not crying, not whimpering either. Daniel squinted at it, looking back at him, just doing that, just looking. Babies did that too.

Flightstaff to landing, something to landing.

Michaela was holding out her hands, the baby dangling, he passed her it.

Then the landing, and the bumps and the rocking and bump bump bump they were down.

The old guy's eyes opened. They had been closed. Maybe he was praying. People prayed. Long flights and they worried. What about? The crash, the plane crashing. Daniel smiled. He reached into the net compartment, lifted out the phone, he began scrolling, and Michaela smiling to him. Daniel nodded. That was them now, the three of them. And the old guy shifted on his seat, trying to see out the window, he couldnt, not from where he was sitting.

Escape: There is None

There on top of a promontory, beyond that gaping hole in the ground lay a unit of thirty times its depth and to either of four sides but in height immeasurable, incalculable.

So where, where!

Answer there was none. I studied the gradient and began the decline, stepping sideways, the small stones and gravel shifting underfoot. I favoured movement, as we do, and was glad to be moving but it was never enough. I heard firstly as screams, this uproar, not screams but shrieks, not shrieks but roars, roars, or uproaring, in my ears this uproaring within my skull and it would not cease at my command. I was in danger and prepared to go to ground when the moment arrived. Now it had and this knowledge was dependable. If I failed to act worse would follow, dangers known, and unknown the consequences, a fatality perhaps, and I was aware, so aware. Even so, and the moment enclosing me I was aloft and too late too late.

From the jaws of escape!

We utter such glibberies. Then captured. Captured in the saying is never straightforward, and my head then, considering them as a civilized people and they were not civilized. I kept this information to myself. Certain thoughts if not illegitimate may become so. The locals and their culture, I offer no examples. In drawing the reference we consider the meaning of civilization. The Greeks had been civilized. Or so we are given to understand.

Those whose interest lies in maintaining the charade, who pull the strings, the puppeteers. I give the concept then find the language. None should reserve contempt. Experience it, convey it, preferably in the moment, its expression.

Yet in this instance it was less than even-handed, in reference to the judgment, perhaps misguided, perhaps essentially so, in deliberation, given my capture, my captors, by reason alone.

This was my essential being yet over it I could not gain control. These were a people beyond all comprehension. This is my appraisal. I offer it to you.

Your Ref HRMP432cB;234QQ

Dear Madam,

You will be aware that when I made the original contact with the Department I imagined, naively, that an upper level of management would attend the matter, acting swiftly to correct what they might argue was an oversight or exception to a just rule. Instead of this someone of inferior rank appears to have been delegated to reply to my original communication, and this individual merely denied all allegations against Departmental employees in the time-honoured fashion. That I too was a Departmental employee has had little or no bearing on the arguments presented. The spokesperson advised me that these were scurrilous allegations and as such a most serious matter. He warned me that if this had been known at the earlier period then also known was the absence of rights pertaining to individuals in these circumstances, that the one followed the other, for these were societal relations and outwith Departmental boundaries. Any such matter was apportioned intellectually as between the Department and myself, and their business alone.

I took action immediately. Firstly I responded to the Official in question. Secondly I advised the Department that I had contacted the city's political representative to our nation's democratically elected Government and asked her to look into the matter. I advised the Department that henceforth I would copy her into all communications.

A few days hence I found myself in receipt of unwarranted and wholly unacceptable advice from yourselves, to the effect that the Department had advised me on several previous occasions that I could not involve persons other than myself and close family members in affairs of this nature. Was I unaware of this situation as the working norm of all relations as between the Department and staff employees?

Imagine my chagrin at the next step in the procedure, when the city's political representative to our nation's democratically elected Government delivered to myself an electronic communication. This arrived courtesy of my personal computer whose internal workings I had assumed sacrosanct. She expressed to me her personal disappointment that for all future skirmishes with the Department I—of necessity—must act alone. She wished me well for the future and trusted that she might rely on my personal support in all subsequent matters pertaining to her position. She asked that she be kept in the loop on a regular basis and that any matter of particular relevance should be conveyed to her not electronically but via overland postal delivery c/o the Northern Regional Office.

Thereafter a Senior Departmental Manager entered the proceedings. He took the leading role in a new line of attack. This amounted to the direct assassination of my character, with callous indifference to my health and well-being. The general treatment now meted out by the Department was accomplished in full and working knowledge of the clinical position. This resulted in the breakdown of the many discrepancies found in the psychological and neurological context whose route to fruition was thought to have finalized several years previously. It had been stressed to them the gravity and likely outcome of the situation. This had been ignored by the Department.

Now with the advent of the Senior Departmental Manager a fresh and cynical campaign against me was mounted. A detailed account of these has been placed in front of the Department on many occasions and scant regard has been paid them.

In every aspect of these proceedings I have provided factual evidence of all matters that have a bearing on the case, as accepted on Departmental authority. This is the factor that would astound any unbiased observer. I have no doubt about that. Even then, and following from this, came the statement masquerading as a finalized document in which the Senior Departmental Manager not only disregarded my respectful blandishments but revealed a signal personalized fury that I should have had "the audacity to intrude in Departmental affairs." I reminded the Senior Departmental Manager that I too was a Departmental employee; and, moreover, in respect of his Seniority, he had a duty to lend caring support to any junior colleagues under attack psychologically, physically and spiritually, and that such was not only factually based but demonstrable and, further, that example upon example littered the historical record.

The intervention of the city's political representative to our nation's democratically elected Government was now alluded to in defence of the Senior Managerial policies, principles and procedures. By her actions she had shewn a fundamental respect for the Department wholly absent from my own personal dealings. What is more her later acquiescence indicated to them the startling puerility of my original assumption, that the city's political representative to our nation's democratically elected Government, should somehow place herself at my personal elbow, and hence "found in my corner rather than theirs," as though we were boxers.

Following this communication, after a lengthy delay, I received a card advising me that the matter had been placed in the hands of Human Resources. This card carried no Departmental source but instead the reference HRMP432cB;234QQ.

Any reference such as this offers clear grounds for an Appeal towards a Just Declaration, under the guidelines, and I hereby advise the Department that a specialist in these matters of fact, highly experienced in all dealings betwixt Citizens and State, has awarded me a clinical opinion held in some quarters to carry more weight than any Departmental declaration and that this will most certainly prove, beyond all reasonable doubt, that any undue and highly severe stress occasioned towards myself is an effect of that primary appellation.

Accordingly, acting under advice, I have charged this city's political representative to our nation's democratically elected Government that my case has now spread to include herself and advisors, in a role I may now define as collusive. I write to you in this first instance to advise the Department that immediate cognisance must be awarded this communication.

Yours faithfully,

HRMP432cB;234QQ

A Time to Come

THE man who was my father was a Minister of the Church
of Christ Jesus who died for our sins. He was nailed to the
Cross of Calvary. I was unlike my father. I did believe in
God who is the Father but not in my father's way, nor that
of the other persuasions.

Others did not so believe and on my behalf, as they
represented, they proposed good things. It was a lie. They
were wrongdoers. Evil people were among them and would
not leave me alone. I would have screamed and would have
screamed louder, screaming at them, I would have screamed
at them.

My life was not wasted. My belief states: to be nailed to
a cross is not the Father for me. Not in my life and lifetime,
my own father was himself in deed, in body, in spirit and I
could have wished for no one more dear.

I only had to think "my life" and already it was happening, shaking the damn thing—my head, already doing it, I
was shaking my damn head. This was the power. Power of
it. What was "it," this power?

Honesty.

I knew what I was.

Honesty.

Failure.

Because it was me. Worse than failure. A failure does
not realize expectations. I had none. I thought of the time
to come and believed in it. Jesus did not let me down. He
was the Godly figure and I knew of my time in the footsteps of my own father there was not the need to prolong

the process. I had thought of necessity which did not apply. There had been a need to prolong it before but not now. I would face it, turn to it, my body there and straight moving, straight standing, how my eyes were downcast but not now, they must not be, but lifted, my head straight, if he is my maker or pater who my maker is to be must have one, have had one, the master is greater than the father. In my head was Jesus, our similarity, as individuals having the traits, those so revealed.

People stopped us from taking part in the crusade but people are always there and always stopping other people. If not we could have joined. My mother would have played a prominent role. I too. I might have. They did not allow it. I thought it unfair but she said otherwise. She said this life is so. I shook my head but did not smile. They might have wished such. I did not. My mother said our time might come. I knew that it would. I knew it always and in her footsteps so too my own time, it too would come.

The Courage to Move

I was there with T who was doing the driving. He had agreed to bring me though with misgivings, which he had yet to voice. He was an acquaintance from way back and didnt have to take anybody anywhere. I sensed his hostility. A pack of cigarettes lay in the side door compartment. I took one. His gaze followed my action.

I just feel like one, I muttered.

He didnt respond. He didnt even shrug, just gazed ahead. Fair enough. I reached for the dashboard lighter. He let down the window when I exhaled smoke. The effect was immediate, the hit on the blood, the oxygen. It was a few weeks since my last. I took two more drags and chucked it out the window. He glimpsed me doing it. I should have explained why I "was wasting" a whole cigarette, but couldnt be bothered.

Thirty more miles. When I spoke he listened, not intently but he did hear: enough to show me that he had no personal interest in the proceedings; it was something to be done and that was that. I had precedence and the thing came first. He accepted this, or wouldnt have been here.

The car had stopped, he remained in it, I strolled to the building. It seemed like a warehouse. Inside there was a room off the lobby; the office. Two women were working at computers. They had expected me and I sat to wait. They showed no interest at first. I realised they were being more than pleasant, but in an odd way they were unsympathetic. Why odd? It was amusing to me. The older woman was looking at me and let me know this is what she was doing.

She had had to shift the way she was sitting to do it. She managed all that without a smile. It was too serious for that. Did I want to pursue this further? It was up to me. She was a very attractive woman. And physically, of course. I realized I wanted to sniff her neck. That was a crazy desire but that was how it was. She still didnt smile. This was strange when I think about it, that my presence did not faze her yet it was this giving rise to this thing, this new thing. She had never seen me before in her life. An odd thought, strange yet enveloping me, man, I was inside of it. No, she had never seen me before but she was relaxed, I saw that she was.

Maybe my being there relaxed her.

Of course I was younger than her but not in too obvious a sense. If that had been the case she never would have looked at me, not in that way.

Now she was frowning. It was time to move. I had been staring. I didnt realise this until I wondered why the frown.

Never mind. I think I sighed, That was it. Nowadays I sighed a lot without realising I was doing it. She was looking at me again. I smiled. I couldnt help it. Life!—what was left of it. I had been nervous, it's true: now I wasnt.

The younger woman was printing off a document and nodded me over when she completed the job. She passed me the document. Just take it through, she said, then returned her attention to the computer.

Another corridor. Some are confused by confrontation. Not me. There's a painting of a corridor done in cubist style, all jaggy dead ends and broken angles, the darkest corners; disguised doors. I walked along. At the end of this one there was a door and a landing and two men at the stairhead. Descending stairs, a basement. So they were guarding the door. It made sense. I showed them the document. They nodded. I was to wait there. They turned their back on me. This was not strange which in itself was strange. But it indicated I was accepted. This alerted me. I was here and could not turn back, not easily, not as a natural form of departure. Could I retreat? I dont know. Maybe not at this level. Decisions such as these are made elsewhere and never behind closed doors.

I had chosen to be here. I had committed myself. This course of action was mine alone. I was under no one's control; no organisational control. Neither state nor global policy guided this course of action. All decisions were mine, and the end result of proper deliberation. I could have been here a full decade ago. It had taken me almost twenty years. This is our time. After a moment the older one looked at me. He was ten years my senior. He grasped my hand and held it for a moment longer than was comfortable. I did not strain to escape him. He sniffed. You smoke? he asked. I shook my head. He was silent for a moment, then nodded. Okay?

Yes, I said, I'm okay.

Good man.

I didnt smile but was glad of the encouragement, slight as it was. Perhaps it wasnt slight. Being this far in brought acceptance if not justification. I doubt if he knew my identity. Perhaps I was wrong, I could have been way wrong. It wouldnt have mattered; here chains of hierarchy were discarded. Parity at last. The older woman was here and I knew she would have been. But was it an expectation? She was stretching out her arm, her right hand, reaching to me. But I didnt trust her, and her face too, the expression on her face. If I had touched her skin, her breast. This would have taken us out of ourselves and this moment, this situation or world, it would have transformed our lives. She would not have stopped my hand. She would have breathed in so sharply, a rasping breath, my fingers on her skin, inching down towards the beautiful surround of her nipple. But the decision was made and would not be rescinded. This to the line of obliteration. We talk about these things, peculiar concepts, such as, for example, death.

Doom. Fate. Nothing.

Between us are parallel actions.

This was the significance of her presence. T was outside in the car. He was no longer pretending indifference, I knew that. His way was calming himself, the attempting so to do, wondering if he might be next.

That was up to him. I didnt care about the two men at the head of the stairs, nor the younger woman who had been by the computer. When she now appeared I was glad to see her. She must have jinked through the corridor. I might have laughed. She was beyond me now. Caution was required. I could do it. I smiled. A strength was there and it was a returning strength. I wondered about T who had remained outside in the car. He was doing the driving and driving was necessary, had been necessary. Not now.

Man 1, 2, 3

The two men following, they thought I hadnt seen them. Of course I had. I knew them because I didnt. I realised that they wanted me to know they were following me. They were allowing it to happen. One had a moustache and I called him Man 1 and he was like a cop, quite heavy set; the other guy smaller and blond headed, quite a good looking guy in a magazine type of way, Man 2.

What did they think I was going to run! Never. This was my place, my streets, my people. I calmed down in the walking then stopped altogether. It was nearby a café with a few customers sitting outside, having a smoke with their coffee. I sat on a chair too and it looked like I was about to chat with somebody except there was no somebody. Man 1 and 2 appeared and kept walking, and on they kept, and along down the main road. I watched them vanish round a corner.

They were dangerous. These people always were. They always are. I knew they would return and got up, I found an empty table inside.

If they came back what would happen? I dont know. But at that stage I thought inside the café was the best bet. They would come back. Maybe they were not interested in me? Who said they were following? Me. How did I know, I didnt. I was only going by why they were there, why on earth. Coming right behind me like that: why else unless they were following. It wouldnt end here.

The woman waiter was watching me.

But if I said to her to watch out for Man 1 and 2 she would worry. Either I was dangerous or else the two men were dangerous; no matter, the situation itself, here lay danger and she would sense this immediately, as had I, and why I was here, here now: she saw me watching her, and I smiled, as though in reassurance.

(He told me this.)

Away to the rear I saw her coming towards us—Lesley I'm talking about. What would I say? Oh jees it was so difficult, just knowing what to say. Oh but I was not of sufficient calibre. My own intelligence, how d'ye call it, for this situation, situations like this, if that is what it was, intelligence. But what else? If I had in the past I could in the future and the now was the future, her coming towards us, oh jees. No, I was incapable, always, that was me. Not admitting the truth because that is what we hide. We hide the truth. I could not move from this situation. Colin was there and if he could and the others too, all of them, so I could too, and I would stand firmly and my gratitude to them, and if so, just if so

but not alone never alone I was not able. Like with Lesley or who, somebody, I worried. How would they respond? I'm talking to her, the authorities? I couldnay prepare for that. These kind of emergencies. Who could? Nobody. Not me anyway.

What is an emergency?

There are these things definitely but not them; too personal, way too personal. I would not speak of such stuff, even if I could, I would resist the temptation. No such talking, mere talking. Why not? Why did I not speak openly, personally? Always holding reins, reins on myself, reining in myself. What did I have to give? Lesley thought

Lesley thought always Lesley thought

that I had the capacity. She thought that I did. This upset me, that I might be capable, that she might think such a thing, that I was, that I could be so, just able to, a just to, to be capable, being capable, she thought that.

It was a shock to realise that I was holding back tears. I turned to walk away, had to, to not be there. But Colin and the others too, who the hell were they looking at were they looking at me, bastards. I walked on myself; a few paces just, pretending interest in whatever, whatever was there, permanent fixtures, featureless.

The others too, how come they were there? Who were they? Could I speak to them? Who the hell were they? Were they even vouched for? People vouch for ye. Who vouched for them? I had the respect for Colin but who the hell were they, fucking bastards. I dont like people that just kinda— they just, they jump in, they jump in. It didnay concern them.

In women there is the additional matters. Not only one thing. All these other qualities. Besides the respect I had for her there was the admiration, she accomplished so much, so so much. Really, and it was all beyond me. That is the beautiful thing and could have me smiling right in the here and how just like wherever I am in whatever situation, whatever it is, how dangerous and how kind, but thoughts of her and

So in this she was correct. Indeed she was. I held this whatever—capacity, to be able. I could. Yes, I could. I was strong and I was fit and I was male. Lesley

oh God.

was not, Lesley was by deed and by thought and oh oh oh, oh God, see her move, how she moved, subtlety of movement, I would be quaking, if I had been one of them, but I was not, I was one of us, and I was so grateful. This upset me. Again the shock, again again again I was holding back tears, these tears, fresh tears. If I had allowed it to happen. and never would I allow such a thing. Never. That would be the emergency, the true emergency, emergency of emergencies.

I had to turn. I could turn, and so walk: if I might crawl then I might walk, fuck you bastards, I was smiling, pretending interest in the

the featureless fixtures, their permanency; the cause, effects.

I did not know who they were. Perhaps I did. Not for certain. I knew Colin and that was for certain. He was one of us and I belonged, I was one of them, he was one of them and the them was where I belonged, but not the others.

Although how did I know? Maybe they were? Were they vouchsafed? Who by? That sensitivity, that was lacking. For such as that sharing was the necessity, that was like solidarity and I did not share it otherwise—I would not be thinking about it. No, not with them. For Lesley, for all women, for every woman. We could not reach to there, therein

The others were talking. Colin too, he was with them. I heard them, and he was one of them. We had turned up for hostility practice that morning, but not as usual; the change had happened. I knew it had. Nothing could be done. This was inevitable. The feel of the hostility, the feel of it, that tangibility. Whohh. Individual traits we had not known to exist. All I could do was resume, and say nothing, show nothing; acknowledge nothing.

Speaking makes trouble, said Colin.

But I didn't like him telling me that. Was he talking about me or simply generalizing? It was one thing or the other. It had to be. He acted like it didnt and gave a gesture so like I was the problem and he had seen this in me and it was to do with Lesley coming towards us, towards me, this woman, so it altered circumstances. Yes it did, oh jees yes, yes yes yes.

Oh okay, said Colin. Here you are again.

I could have smiled but didnt. Yes. That was me again, I was not giving in. I stared at him. I was comfortable. It didnt matter about them, the others, they could do whatever, what they wanted to do, why didnt they just do it. I took it from Colin, not from them.

I'm just getting at you, he said, you open your mouth and you talk, what is talk, talk is not cheap, you make it cheap; cheep cheep, you are a canary. You put us all at risk. You think it is only Lesley, it is not only Lesley.

I saw an apology. I didnt. I was not about to. I didnt feel that. Behind him and the others I saw Lesley now seeing me and staring straight at me, into me and inside, beyond. I dont know as if. She did not waver, seeing that I saw, she saw me, seeing me, she was seeing me and she saw me as able, I was able.

I always knew that Colin was fooling me, but there were times I chose to suppose something else and I do not know why.

They say the future looks strongly in our favour but beyond that who knows. Who knows if ever we can proceed beyond it. That was what they said. The absurdity of such a thought never had occurred to me until now. Beyond the future. A time beyond time.

This is the stage I had reached. My head was full of struggle, the struggle. What is the difference, if there is one. Who might answer? Nobody.

There is no end is a plausible answer. I should have learned that early. Nothing lies beyond the struggle. Lesley knew about these matters. Colin too. I was never alone and should not have thought in that way. Through tiredness we fight and through pain; we cross barriers. I dug my forefingernail into my brow, drawing blood from a scratch to keep myself from falling into sleep.

That was later. Colin had boiled water and made coffee, weak coffee, coffee junior we called it, water weak. He was forcing conversation; basic procedure. He had a laugh talking about old stuff. I listened and observed, observed Lesley.

The conversation was necessary and I needed it. Deeds encountered, wherein the hero, should he drop into slumber, the world become alien. I needed not to, to fall into slumber, my head was gone. I did not know why anything, why me why family, friend—solidarity, what the hell was that? solidarity, where women are. Solidarity as against women? Meaningful words for meaningless concepts. I did not know any longer.

Colin passed me the mug of the coffee and carried on with his stories from childhood, our childhood which we shared. But this was twenty-five years on from that. This knowledge set a grim, a grimness. This was our situation. I could not break my own attachments, respect for authority, the pathos. That was me. I recognised myself in Colin's ever watchful observance. Perhaps it was my father. A stern man. I think of him now. Humourless man. I think about him. He did not smack children. The look, his look, looking at you and when you see he is seeing, and his seeing. This is what you see and it was enough, always enough. But not here. Here was our present. There was nothing beyond. Except Lesley was there, she was within and always beyond, always beyond, and I could make that leap

I waited now, if he wished to speak further I would have listened. He didnt. Eventually I was alone. This was the morning. There was that shift in the sky, parting movement, parting glance, and I saw now another was there. He stood by me. He had to stand by me.

I was sitting down, fair enough. I knew he was there. Not who he was. It was his duty. But we all have duties, obligations. I had the need to speak. That was my duty. I had learned from the experience and there was no going back.

So, the big question: was this my confession? He would never know but he would have wondered.

Nobody else was there to hear. That is what happens. That is life.

If no one was there I would not have spoken, so I know for sure. I started talking so he heard me. It was unavoidable. He had ears. I could have reached out and touched him, if such had been possible. In this life there is the possible. We look for the possible and act accordingly, or at least try.

Mates a Long Time

Me and Jimmy were mates a long time. It was disappointing to hear he had died. Disappointing does not sound strong enough, yet there isnt a better.

"How are ye disappointed by somebody dying?" is a fair question. One tries to answer it. A guy like Jimmy. There wasnay much went by him, at least there didnay used to be. Towards the end there was and it was a nuisance, and I am saying "it" and not "he."

I am choosing my words carefully. I know the family. Questions were being asked. I am talking about him. I had nay problem personally and I dont think he had, no with that. He was aye a confident buggar. Except when his girl-friend came into it, if ye can say "girlfriend." That was the point and that was the problem. I saw him fuck off a couple of times, just at the mention of her name. I'm talking leaving a company, he just left; up he got and that was that. Ye were standing at the bar with him, couple of guys, pals, and somebody happens to say it: Oh I saw Clare the other day.

Just her name, that was that and that was him: drink up, time to go.

Women have nice names. I said that to him once. He never forgot it and never forgave me. We had a row about it. It wasnay funny. That fundamental jealousy, even the word "woman" was tricky. Take nothing for granted. There isnay a safe way. I saw him staring at me once, and I genuinely believe he was waiting to see if I would give the game away. Even if I smiled, he would read it like a smirk. Naw, it certainly was not funny. That deadpan way he had, that could be scary. I'm saying that and I was what ye would call "close," a "close pal." Aye, I'll say it, Jimmy was scary.

Now he's dead okay, I will say it—Clare, a good look-ing woman, a sexy woman. And in a quiet way she knew it. One of these women I dont think even likes men, not when it comes down to it. A lot of them dont, they just put up with ye. The difference is too massive. Mair like another species. Ye try and work it out. It's a hard one. Guys dont take ye up on it. It's a conundrum. "What has testoster-one got to do with smelly socks?" is a fair question. I could imagine a woman asking that though I never heard it said. Sometimes a guy said it, or said something like it, and we would all smile. It happened at the funeral and it was a spluttering-into-the-beer scenario. If one of us had laughed everybody would have laughed, fucking raucous. People in the pub all looking at ye, some with a quiet smile, others naw, daggers. We managed to avoid it. There's folk dont like a crowd of guys laughing. What are they laughing at? What if it is you, if they're laughing at you, you're the target? A different kettle of fish. Folk don't like it. Plus funerals. Ye're supposed to be remembering the dead party. Except it was Jimmy, if it wasnay for him naybody would have laughed in the first place, it wouldnay have been that funny. It was him made it funny. People forget.

We were in at the club lounge, where the refreshments were on the tables. A black tie and shirt affair, except for the young squad: Jimmy's grandkids and all that. Nayn of them know how to dress. Good on them. What's appropriate and what isnay. Who cares, they dont know, and so what. They wouldnay mind ye laughing.

No just them, other folk too. Women. Oh it's just a bunch of men, that is what women would say. That would sum it up. Who knows what they laugh about. Who knows anything about them. That is how women would see it. If ye were a comic ye could use it for a stand-up routine, the male female divide: first question to the audience, testosterone, et cetera, if ye knew how to spell it—even saying that would get a laugh, a snigger. Except ye would have to mind the punchline and sometimes I couldnay.

He was a huffy cunt too. If ever ye interrupted him; telling ye a story, if he didnay get the chance of finishing it. That look he gave ye. It was a row, if ye werenay paying attention. Ye were goni say something to him till ye saw the look, and that way he stared at ye. Like I said, we were mates a long time, but ye see that look and ye wonder. So ye raise the glass. A silent *sláinte*. In and out yer life. A world of stuff vanishing. Where did the years go? Years and minutes. What does it even mean?

And if Frogs could speak they would have a sore throat

I once contacted an emissary of an eminent publishing house on the advice of a well-wisher. Said emissary met me in a bar in the downtown reaches of a certain metropolis. He may or may not have been an emissary but he was a freeloading bastard. He was bored with my company after the first several rounds of booze, all of which I had bought. He was toying with the dregs; dregs of the first, dregs of the second, dregs of the third. It irritated me greatly. I hate dregs. I cannay abide them. Where I come from there are no dregs. Ye fucking swally a pint and that is that, one buys another, and holds the hour. I asked in tones of the weightiest irony if he might care for a fourth.

Sir you are too kind, too kind, is this a trait of your nation?

Aye across yer fucking skull ya fucking prick. I controlled, however, one's pique, and bought him the fourth. I noticed he was peering across the bar. At himself! In the gantry mirror! He wasnay so much peering as preening. He managed to resist gieing himself the glad-eye. Ya bampot bammy bastard, I whispered to myself in tones of subdued passion. I had become interested in myself as specimen qua specimen and paused to speculate. Why was I doing it? What kind of numbskull fucking masochistic fool was I! Or was it a national characteristic? Walk all over me. I beg of you. Trample me into the earth. Oblivion here I come. Fuck the Pope while we're at it. Or should it be the Defender of the Englishers, the faith, aye, well fuck him too?

This present situation was of massive psychological import. Here I was in straits of impecunial desperation. I had borrowed money for this literary jaunt into the sophisticated jungle of the upper downtown area. It was mid evening and I had no place to stay.

This is true. I had nowhere to stay! And my only excuse for this long game I appeared to be playing, kidding myself on as per fucking usual but which part of me was sleeping it rough for christ sake.

I had had it in mind that this publisher's emissary might have booked me into a room of some exclusive, members-only club to which I had been led to believe he was taking me, via the paths of booze and general unrighteousness. Instead of which here we were in some damn boring genteel dump of a place, all retired Military generals and exiled members of Near and Middle Eastern Aristocracies, fucking shahs and sheikhs, this guy was taking me to nay place bar the cleaners. I was goni have to phone a friend, an old buddy of mine and this time of night is not conducive to old buddies, especially married ones with weans. Luckily—or should it be unluckily?—he was a stalwart of the left and short in temper in the company of rightwing fascist bastards of which the countries I inhabit abound, through no fault of my own I hasten to add and would hope that he might accept such in mitigation.

And now the freeloading emissary bastard had his latest beer raised to his chin. Your good health kind sir, he said.

And I knew I was fukt. I marvelled at myself, then was aware of a twitch in my left eye, it was uncontrollable, uncontrollable. I sniffed, and that catch in the upper larynx, the short cough, clearing of the throat, the croaking. Oh man, man, how do we cope, our own cowardliness, our subjection, our fucking shit-covered intellects, shite-filled brains, yes sir no sir three fucking bags fucking full of fucking the worst forms of excremental

bla bla.

Snow-Monkeys

The first full day of my own engagement was the Friday of all Fridays, ending with the Individual. Following on from that was the Event of the Eight Visitations which required four participants from the audience. Unbeknown to myself events were switched and each was to have taken place the previous afternoon and evening. I was shocked. None of the organizers had forewarned me. How could such a mistake have happened? Later I discovered they were volunteers and hardly knew anything. I was left without an appetite.

When this was regained I resisted all food placed in front of me. I hoped thus to strengthen my emotional range. This nowadays appears a general position although I have never grasped why. I was not in the best physical state. Unfortunately this expressed itself in a sustained loss of that looser form of spiritual temper which I found necessary to a proper performance, avoiding the psychological mal-adjustments effected by my oversensitivity to class affronts. The reaction to this surprised me. My audience appeared to assume I was engaged in an irony of which they were unfamiliar.

Overnight a heavy fall of snow occurred. The weather had turned very cold. The organizers let it be known that those of us who wished to take advantage of this might remain indoors. I thought this unprofessional but had brought several books with me.

I became, if not acquainted with the Hotel Staff, at least identifiably present to them and was given suitable shoes to get about the gardens. These shoes reminded me of paddles.

I said as much to the staff member who supplied them. He bowed respectfully.

One morning, I closed a book, donned the paddles and set off on a walk. The Hotel Staff had cleared a passageway through the deep snow. Soon I bumped into a pack of overly curious snow-monkeys. I had only ever seen them on television; nature programmes. I was about to clap one when it occurred to me that I would not clap a polar bear or a snow-leopard so why a snow-monkey? Were they even domesticated? And if they were so said to be, was this information reliable, or designed for tourists and visiting performers?

I would have preferred to avoid such an encounter but the thought flashed through my mind that there was a positive side to it. This was a form of structural excuse that would allow me to skip more than half of the Heavenly Music section that brought to an end the Event of the Eight Visitations. The snow-monkeys were by now swivelling, crossing and dropping from the tops of the high, walled enclosures. Somehow I was amused to see them. I laughed in the hope that this might appease them while reaching to secure the straps of my snow-shoes, perhaps to outrun them, perhaps to glide my way clear, I could not be certain, but all was not lost.

The one with the dog

What I fucking do is wander about the place, just going here and there. I've got my pitches. A few other cunts use them as well. They keep out my road cause I lose my temper. I've got two mates I sometimes meet up with to split for a drink and the rest of it. Their pitches are out the road of mine. One of them's quiet. That suits me. The other yin's a gab. I'm no that bothered. What I do I just nod. If anybody's skint it'll be him. He's fucking hopeless. The quiet yin's no bad. I quite like the way he does it. He goes up and stares into their eyes. That's a bit like me except I'll say something. Give us a couple of bob. The busfare home. That kind of thing. It doesnt fucking matter. All they have to do is look at you and they know the score. What I do I just stand waiting at the space by the shops. Sometimes you get them with change in their hands; they've no had time to stick it back into their purses or pockets. Men's the best. Going up to women's no so hot because they'll look scared. The men are scared as well but it's no sexual and there's no the same risks with the polis if you get clocked doing it. Sometimes I feel like saying to them give us your jacket ya bastard. It makes me laugh. I've never said it yet. I dont like the cunts and I get annoyed. Sometimes I think ya bastard ye I'm fucking skint and you're no. It's a mistake. It shouldnt fucking matter cause you cant stop it. There's this dog started following me. It used to go with that other yin, the quiet cunt. It tagged behind him across in the park one morning and me and the gab told him to fucking dump it cause it must belong to somebody but he didnt fucking bother, just shrugs. One thing I'm finding but

181

it makes it a wee bit easier getting a turn. But I dont like it
following me about. I dont like that kind of company. I used
to have a mate like that as well, followed me about and that
and I didnt like it. I used to tell him to fuck off. That's what
I sometimes do with the dog. Then sometimes they see you
doing it and you can see them fucking they dont like it, they
dont like it and it makes them scared at the same time. I'd
tell them to fuck off as well. That's what I feel like doing
but what I do I just ignore them. That's what I do with the
dog too, cause it's best. Anything else is daft, it's just getting
angry and that's a mistake. I try no to get angry; it's just
the trouble is I've got a temper. That's what the gab says
as well, your trouble he says you've got a fucking temper,
you're better off just taking it easy. But I do take it easy. If
they weigh you in then good and if they dont then there's
always the next yin along. And even if you dont get a turn
the whole fucking day then there's always the other two and
usually one of them's managed to get something. That's the
good thing about it, having mates. What I dont understand
I dont understand how you get a few of the cunts going
about in wee teams, maybe four or five to a pitch, one trying
for the dough while the rest hang about in the background.
That's fucking hopeless cause it just puts them off giving
you anything and sometimes you can even see them away
crossing the street just to keep out the way, as if they're
fucking scared they're going to get set about if they dont
cough up. It's stupid as well cause there's always some cunt
sees what you're up to and next thing the polis is there and
you're in fucking bother. What I think I think these yins that
hang about in the background it's cause they're depressed.
They've had too many knockbacks and they cant fucking
take it so what they do they start hanging about with some
cunt that doesnt care and they just take whatever they can
get. If it was me I'd just tell them to fuck off; away and fuck
I'd tell them, that's what I'd say if it was me.

Getting Outside

I'll tell you something: when I stepped outside that door I was alone, and I mean alone. And it was exactly what I had wanted, almost as if I'd been demanding it. And that was funny because it's not the kind of thing I would usually demand at all; usually I didnt demand anything remotely resembling being outside that door. But now. Christ. And another thing: I didnt even feel as if I was myself. What a bloody carry on it was. I stared down at my legs, at my trousers. I was wearing these corduroy things I mostly just wear to go about. These big bloody holes they have on the knee. So that as well. Christ, I began to think my voice would start erupting in one of these bloodcurdling screams of horror. But no. Did it hell, I was in good control of myself. I glanced down at my shoes and lifted my right foot, kidding on I was examining the shoelaces and that, to see if they were tied correctly. One of those stupid kind of things you do. It's as if you've got to show everybody that nothing's taking place out the ordinary. This is the kind of thing you're used to happening. It's a bit stupid. But the point to remember as well; I was being watched. It's the thing you might forget. So I just I think sniffed and whistled a wee bit, to kid on I was assuming I was totally alone. And I could almost hear them drawing the curtains aside to stare out. Okay but I thought: here I am alone and it's exactly what I wanted; it was what I'd been demanding if the truth's to be told. I'll tell you something as well: I'm not usually a brave person but at that very moment I thought Christ here you are now and what's happening but you're keeping on going, you're keeping on going, just as if you couldnt give a damn about who was watching. I'm not kidding you I felt as great as ever I've felt in my whole life, and that's a fact. So much so I was beginning to think is this you that's doing it. But it bloody was me, it was. And then I was walking and I mean walking, just walking, with nobody there to say yay or nay. What a feeling thon was. I stopped a minute to look about. An error. Of course, an error. I bloody knew it as soon as I'd done it. And out they came.

Where you off to?

Eh—nowhere in particular.

Can we come with you?

You?

Well we feel like a breath of fresh air.

I looked straight at them when they said that. It was that kind of daft thing people can say which gives you nearly nothing to reply. So I just, what I did for a minute, I just stared down at my shoes and then I said, I dont know how long I'll be away for.

They nodded. And it was a bit of time before they spoke back. You'd prefer we didnt come with you. You want to go yourself.

Go myself?

Yes, you prefer to go yourself. You dont want us to come with you.

No, it's not that, it's just, it's not that, it's not that at all, it's something else.

They were watching me and not saying anything.

It's just I dont know how long I'll be away. I might be away a couple of hours, there again I might be away till well past midnight.

Midnight?

Yes, midnight, it's not that late surely, midnight, it's not that late.

We're not saying it is.

Yes you are.

No we're not.

But you are, that's what you're saying.

We arent. We arent saying that at all. We're not caring at all what you do. Go by yourself if you like. If you had just bloody told us to begin with instead of this big smokescreen you've always got to draw this great big smokescreen.

I have not.

Yes you have. That's what you've done.

That's what I'd done. That's what they were saying: they were saying I'd drawn this great big smokescreen all so's I could get outside the door as if the whole bloody carry on was just in aid of that. I never said anything back to them. I just thought it was best waiting and I just kind of kidded on I didnt really know what they were meaning.

Roofsliding*

The tenement building upon which the practice occurs is of the three-storey variety. A section of roof bounded on both sides by a row of chimney stacks is favoured. No reason is known as to why this particular section should be preferred to another. Certain members of the group participating are thought to reside outwith this actual building though none is a stranger to the district. Roofsliding, as it is termed, can take place more than once per week and will always do so during a weekday mid morning. As to the season of the year, this is unimportant; dry days, however, being much sought after.

The men arise in single file from out of the rectangular skylight. They walk along the peak of the roof ensuring that one foot is settling on either side of the jointure which is bevelled in design, the angle at the peak representing some 80 degrees. During the walk slates have been known to break loose from their fixtures and if bypassing the gutter will topple over the edge of the building to land on the pavement far below. To offset any danger to the public a boy can always be seen on the opposite pavement, from where he will give warning to the pedestrians.

When the men, sometimes designated roofsliders, have assembled along the peak they will lower themselves to a

---

* This account has been taken more or less verbatim from a pamphlet entitled *Within Our City Slums*; it belongs to the chapter headed "Curious practices of the Glaswegian." The pamphlet was published in 1932 but is still available in a few secondhand bookshops in the south of England.

sitting posture on the jointure, the legs being outstretched flatly upon the sloped roof. They face to the front of the building. Roofsliding will now commence. The feet push forward until the posterior moves off from the jointure onto the roof itself, the process continuing until the body as a whole lies prone on the gradient at which point momentum is effected.

Whether a man "slides" with arms firmly aligned to the trunk, or akimbo, or indeed lying loosely to the sides, would appear to be a function of the number of individuals engaged in the activity at any given period (as many as thirty-two are said to have participated on occasion). Legs are, however, kept tightly shut. When the feet come to rest on the gutter roofsliding halts at once and the order in which members finish plays no part in the practice.

A due pause will now occur. Afterwards the men manoeuvre themselves inch by inch along the edge of the roof while yet seeming to maintain the prone position. Their goal, the line of chimney stacks that stand up right to the northside of the section. From here the men make their way up to the join-ture on hands and knees. It is worth noting that they do so by way of the outside, unwilling, it would appear, to hazard even the slightest damage to the "sliding" section that is bounded between here and the line of chimney stacks to the southside. When all have gathered on the jointure once again they will be seated to face the rear of the building. Now and now only shall conversation be entered upon. For up until this period not a man amongst them shall have spoken (since arrival by way of the skylight).

At present a ruddy complexioned chap in his forty-fourth year is the "elder statesman" of the roofsliders. Although the ages do vary within the group no youth shall be admitted who has yet to attain his fourteenth birthday. On the question of alcohol members are rightly severe, for not only would the "wrong doer" be at mortal risk, so too would the lives of each individual.

As a phenomenon there can be no doubt as to the curious nature of the practice of roofsliding. Further observation might well yield fruits.

That thread

After the pause came the other pause and it was the way
they have of following each other the next one already in
its place as if the sequence was arranged according to some
design or other, and set not just by the first but them all,
a networked silence. It was that way when she entered
the room. The noise having ceased right enough but even
allowing for that if it hadnt it would have—which is usually always the case. She had the looks to attract, a figure
exactly so, her sensuousness in all the moves so that her
being there in this objectified way, the sense of a thousand
eyes. Enter softly enter softly: it was like a song he was sing-
ing, and her smile brief, yet bravado as well, that style some
women have especially, the face, the self-consciousness; and
all of them being there and confronting her while her just
there taking it, standing there, one arm down, her fingers
bent, brushing the hem of her skirt. She was not worried
by virtue of him, the darkness of the room, any of it. Like a
sure knowledge of her own disinterest, his nonexistence as
a sexual being, in relation to her, and he grinned, reaching
for the whisky and pouring himself one, adding a half again
of water, the whisky not being a good one. She was still
standing there, as if dubiously. She was seeking out faces
she recognised and his was one that she did recognise, lo,
but would barely acknowledge, she would never acknowledge. Had he been the only face to recognise; the only one.
Even that. He smiled then the sudden shift out from his
side jacket pocket with the lighter and snap, the flare in
the gloom, the thin exhalation of blue smoke; he sipped

at the whisky and water, for his face would definitely have
had to be recognised now, from the activity, no matter how
softly, softly and quietly, no matter how he had contrived it.
Now his elation was so fucking strong, so fucking vivid man,
and striking, and so entirely fucking wonderful he wanted
to scream he had to scream he really did have to he had to
scream he would have to he wouldnt be able to fucking stop
himself he was shaking he was shaking the cuff of his sleeve,
the cuff of his sleeve, trailing on the surface of the table,
his hand shaking, shaking, now twitching and his breath
coming deep, and she would have sensed it, sensed it all,
and she would be smiling so slightly around the corners of
her mouth, the down there, her thick lower lip how round
it was, how round it was and mystifying, to describe it as
provocative was an actual error, an error, a mistake. But the
hesitancy in her movement. That thread having been long
flung out now, though still exploratory, but ensnaring, it
was ensnaring, causing her to hold there, so unmistakably
hesitant now rubbing her shoulder just so self-aware yet in
that kind of fashion a woman has of rubbing her shoulder
at the slightest sensory indication of the thread, feeling it
cling, that quiver and he shivered, raising the whisky to his
mouth and sipping it, keeping his elbow hard in to the side
of his body, keeping it firmly there because that sickness
in the pit of his belly and the blood coursing through his
cheeks, and burning, burning, everyone seeing and knowing, he was so transparent, so transparent, she just shook
her head. What was she going to do? She just had shaken
her head that most brief way, and she turned on her heel
and she left, left him there. He couldnt move. He would cry
out. But his face was controlled, so controlled, although the
colour now drained from his cheeks, or else the opposite,
was it the opposite? and his hand now shaking, the cigarette
lighter on the coffee table.

ULPI NON REUM

The Unities and Loyal Prerogative Initiative (ULPI) was a year-long project, designed for the use of world-wide local authorities. Applications for the ULPI title were available in all countries where the unifying voice is English or may so become English. The project operated in quasi-tangentiality to the US-UK cultural outreach services, bringing to fruition older "in-practice" projects based on standard Business-Cultural Human-Resource models, taking their lead from Sappy Targets NW whose geo-national completist approach has led outreach field strategies in recent times. Their Capital Council of World-English was the birthing model of earlier cultural and community developments, including Dramatic Fields of Trans-Africa, All-American Needles and Arts, and Inter-Asian Force-Fields of Pattern and Colour. The participation of Sappy Targets NW ensures the necessary simultaneity, consistent with identified impulse needs.

Banks, businesses, media and charitable organisations were welcome partners in the ULPI project. Nominated regions were guaranteed full global exposure.

The ULPI Founding Committee had as its working title Creative Unities and the Loyal Prerogative. This might have been allowed but for former Colonial and Secondary English-language colleagues who pushed for the exchange of Loyal for Royal and the reconsideration of the use of the term "Creative." This was dealt with sympathetically by the ULPI Committee. NATO-approved monarchies are apolitical and acceptable in most contemporary settings and our colleagues presented a valid case in favour of the "Royal" appellation. They were praised for this by the Organising Committee. It was agreed that in times of harnessed enthusiasm national differences may be set aside for symbols of a unifying and universal application, and public exclamations of awed submission are among the more satisfactory of these. In areas requiring less formalized procedures oppositional factors may be voiced, albeit in more muted tones. The judicious application of Social State Media is foremost in this. The space occupied by certain approved Royalties may well "equate to that of the Dalai Lama or Pope, rather than the Emperors of Japan or Ethiopia" but the President of the United States, after all, is a man among men.

None needs reminding that democracy in spirit is a key concept in the Creative Unities and the Loyal Prerogative Initiative. Former Colonial and Secondary English-language colleagues were advised that public fora are inappropriate areas for primary exchanges. Whereas propositions grounded on the a priori rights of Elite Leaderships are to be trumpeted in some quarters easy forms of triumphalism are not applauded by the ULPI Committee. Post-Reformation religious writings, lyric and prosaic, may adopt quasi-antirepublican sentiments as a position, but the Committee reminded colleagues that a position held is no premise and none should have qualms in this regard. Even so, and finally, the Organising Committee moved to adopt the rather less flamboyant "Loyal" which was agreed to offer a wider inclusivity. Secretary to the Committee conveyed our respect and appreciation to our former Colonial and Secondary English-language colleagues. Their concerns were noted.

Formal submissions for the Unities and Loyal Prerogative Initiative began two years prior to final selection. Informal procedures had begun earlier than that. Social and Cultural Officers (SACOs) were quickly aligned and in position through multivarious networking routines, moving freely between national regionalities competing for the title. Education and academic institutions were offered assurances that any referential curricula would be defined strictly as under their own auspices and given restricted time-scales. The exigencies of the regional "voice" and its pseudo-indigenous patterns were given full consideration. Our ULPI programme offers a catch-all. Associate members were encouraged to offer a fuller persuasion to individual creatives and thought-provokers, urging them not to remain aloof but to enter into the spirit of the initiative. Further advice was offered in regard to our bursary-award schemes. Tutoring roles, mentoring roles, and fuller residency appointments are also available to those who fulfil the criteria. Award-winning recipients should note that these roles and posts may be self-funding enterprises should they so desire.

During the whittling period between the production of the long and eventual short lists, SACOs of diverse administrations were encouraged to market their nominees thematically for a twenty-four-month period that might link to the theme The Practice of Unitary English and Greatness as Given. The Committee were greatly encouraged by the number and quality of applications received. These arrived from every part of the globe. The Committee liaised with representative authorities, compared proposals, selected several. This was followed by the statutory seven-day festival of creative and arts events which take place prior to final selection.

SACOs were appointed to oversee a multitude of popular events in towns, villages and hamlets. The eventual long list comprised regions of the United Kingdom, North America, Ireland, Canada, Israel, Saudi Arabia, Australia, Qatar, India, Bahrain, New Zealand and an undisclosed number of informal recipients. Of the applications rejected at this long-list level, fringe projects were established and encouraged and will be developed in South-East Asia, the

West Indies, north-west Canada, central and southern Africa, the Indian Sub-Continent and in the Middle and Near East. The experience gained by these subaltern formations will ensure stronger applications in the future. In the interim period it is recommended that our Social and Cultural Officers visit these and other embryonic areas with a view to establishing time-line spikes of indigenous excellence along lines pre-established.

SACOs and delegates from the long-listed regions performed presentations of why theirs should have been chosen. Guests to the home of the Unities and the Loyal Prerogative Initiative programme included popular and classical musicians; actors and sporting heroes; media broadcasters and accredited professionals from the relevant bodies. It has been suggested that for future occasions some among such events should not take place behind closed doors. The lists of oral raconteurs offering individual presentations were outstanding, reminding us of the power of laughter in the spirit of rebellion and individuality. Invited guests were hugely entertained under the amused eye of our ever-watchful patrons and principal benefactors. If the performance of these presentations was a viable yardstick then vast numbers of individual initiative devotees have ahead of them a magnificent year-long treat.

The Secretary to the Committee reminds all stakeholders that we take the Triple-A position: adherence, advocacy and advance. The Secretary confirms that every thought-provoker, individual or general creative is first and foremost a human being and entitled to his or her own individual project. Freedom of expression was never under threat from ourselves, rather was it our mantra. Several of those of award-winning stature accepted our invitation to hold key residencies during the twelve-month period. This was unconditional. Our hope was that the submission of a final report, as comprehensive as one deemed appropriate, would have been forthcoming. An awareness of particular obligations is integral to the nature of our thought-provoker fraternity. This was the hope—indeed expectation—of the Organising Committee, and the majority complied with our wish.

It was hoped that our tutors, mentors and resident creatives would embrace key residencies in a spirit of energy, enthusiasm and cross-societal availability. We had prepared for a variety of responses and were not disappointed. Nor did we suppress our delight at the epic nature of the more skilful contributions. The wonder of humanity is our diversity and of that there is no question. It is always a challenge.

Mr Howard Gerald-Brooke was among those who chose to submit their report in a series of verse chronicles. We welcomed all such reports. Howard's was more than welcome in view of his personal and properly provocative perspective which is diverse, albeit relational. Clearly his was an intensive programme. The Secretary to the Organising Committee proposed that his participation would provide a gateway to areas cerebral and radical otherwise peripheral. This proved to be the case. Howard has held quasi-cognitive posts in earlier formations, thus were we prepared for certain inevitabilities. Suffice it to say our "Expectations" were indeed the "Greater" based on earlier acquaintance. In recent years his war "against the grain" has been one of attrition. Howard is a noted individualist in most areas of provokery but is entitled to comply with intelligence quotients and diktats. This he bore with an admirable calm, and his slogan that All-Thought-Is-Art-Anyway evinced widespread interest within the Committee.

During the residencies he and other participants kept both diary and journal, and recorded much else. The majority of the pieces contained therein—the chronicles, anecdotes, diatribes, digressions and tutorials—are thought to derive from these sources. Some appear distended or otherwise altered as to render them appropriate to the singular projects of the Thought-Provokers. The Organising Committee applauds such diversity and finds room for it. It was acknowledged that for some this represents a quandary. If a form of infinity is accepted as a foundation of Art in-itself then this will bode well for career and contractual prospects but art as individual enterprise will lie outwith the grasp of the specialist.

Yet the proposition that intelligence is of infinite extension remains unchallenged in the view of the Organising Committee. Our use of the concept Inventive Thinking is here realized as an aid to resolving several pedagogical dilemmas. Academics, teachers and other interested parties may rest secure that the value of thought is neither relative nor yet couched in mystery, and never within the auspices of the Unities and Loyal Prerogative Initiative.

Without adequate fiscal control infinite extension is disadvantageous and none would dispute this. The Organising Committee accepts that thought and its expression is also a business, and if on occasion it more resembles a shambling, shapeless edifice then it too must be considered functional and subject to practical restraints. This in response to the misgivings expressed by the professional business community in regard to the edifice, so-called, if it should be too ill-defined to market.

Members of the Organising Committee had met and been impressed at the personal levels of commitment evinced by Mr Howard Gerald-Brooke and friends, anticipated in participatory contexts on separate national and international occasions; predictable perhaps, but not inevitable.

Their visions of a possible future were always of interest in reference to long-term strategies. We regret that those who were unable to conclude the remaining days of their contracted period thought secrecy the better form of leavetaking. Their overall commitment has been a major consideration of those who argued for the rightful nullification of the pertinent parts of the agreement. Should the author of a controversial work be excluded on the grounds of controversy? We thought not. There are no grounds for exclusion. This is our strength. Our many mansions are all-embracing, reflecting the global unity of our ULPI project. The Committee, however, wish Mr Howard Gerald-Brooke and friends continued success in their future enterprises. The amorphity of Human Initiative was acknowledged by the foresighted few as a positive aspect, a paradigm of the financial market itself. They saw the synergetic consequence of this marriage as between Inventive Thought narratives reinforced by eco-political exigency that might render as a member each and all citizens of each and every region that applied for nomination, regardless of point of origin. The overall project may begin in such freedom but all the better to snatch or determine a security, which is key to the ULPI vision. Thought-provokers and individual creatives are certainly exceptional. We make them the rule.

Timothy Signal-Onzire
Acting Director
ULPI NON REUM

Authority and Consolation

I was thinking about my mother's position and found it quite peculiar. There were five of us boys. No girls. I was the second oldest. She had hoped for a girl when I was born. It wasnt my fault I was a boy. Nor was it my mother's. When the nurse showed her the new-born baby it was me: here I was. She and my father had produced a being who answered to the name, Me. It was Me. I was the product.

I was thinking about my father and the position he occupied. Once in the living room the five of us boys were playing a game. It was noisy and quite rumbustious, I would say fairly so. He grabbed one of us older ones by the scruff of the neck. *Father! It wasnt me!* was the cry. *It was you*, said our father. So one of us was punished. Our father beat him. His youngest son did not understand what was happening. He began crying and ran to find our mother who was in the kitchen area. She comforted the boy by stroking his head and shoulders, murmuring to him that he shouldnt worry. The second youngest had stayed in the living room it was horrible seeing a big brother being punished running from the room, finally, straight ben the kitchen to tell his mother, and she listened.

Back in the living room an older boy watched his brother being punished a bit longer then he too left the room. After the beating, amid a series of chokes, the boy who had been beaten blurted out, *Oh Father, it wasnt me.* Our father didnt reply but nodded in an ambivalent manner. He stepped to the window and gazed into the distance.

His eldest son was still watching. Now he turned and left the room. The one who had been punished stopped crying, wiped his face, and followed him. The two youngest were by then in their own space, lying together on the floor watching television. I think our mother was still in the kitchen.

Soon afterwards we older boys were elsewhere, neither together nor apart, just getting on with things. We did not discuss what had happened.

Nowadays, as a grandfather, I think about this episode and see much to consider. Denying culpability began the episode. A brief search for justice was triggered but did not develop, and was never resolved. There was no need for this to be resolved. Justice did not prevail and perhaps justice could not prevail.

The situation might have been described as "unjust," that an "injustice" had taken place, but was that the case? Maybe it was not an injustice. Do we distinguish between minor and major injustices? What is a normal injustice? Can the same incident be both just and unjust?

We hear of an injustice, and respond emotionally. We need to do something and we do it. We throw our weight in support of the victim. Or else we dont. We reflect on the situation. Speedy actions can save the day. Hasty actions can ruin the day.

There are other considerations. A response is not so much necessary as inescapable: helping or not; reflecting on the situation, considering other modes of action, passing by.

Our knowledge of the world begins from shared experience. We make sense of the world in the presence of other human beings. Maybe once we check it out we find that nobody was to blame, or all. Perhaps the entire five boys were culpable. Maybe one of us had been scapegoated, a regular enough occurrence in larger families and how each of us copes is a measure of something, I know not what, except that our mother knew more than most.

I see now that whether or not an injustice had prevailed was never relevant as far as mother was concerned. She had a role and she performed it the best she could. She comforted the youngest and listened to the case as presented by the second youngest: and to each she was offering consolation. None for the older sons, there was none to give. They were developing, and forms of consolation were singular; each dealt with injustice as they followed or made a path.

Empathy was evident all the way through the episode, between every family member, including mother and father. When injustice occurs and we know this to be the case, we perceive solidarity. The more experienced we are the more we come to understand that solidarity may not be the route to universal change. In specific instances it may be the likeliest but there are other considerations.

Our father was authority personified. He relied on our mother for consolation. She knew that he had to make difficult decisions, and punishments were to be exercised warranted or otherwise. He also relied on us older boys. Authority existed and within our home his it was. Thus we learned to accept authority where shown as unjust, where justice was not at issue.

Some cultures and social settings offer other-worldly answers to the matter of higher authority; the existence of external forces, and other-worldly beings who may be physical, spiritual or metaphysical. The Devil may well have been a metaphysical being but (he) could produce physical results, sometimes with the aid of non-human beings who could bestride the physical and metaphysical, such as demons and fallen angels, and others too.

When mothers are unavailable the authority personified appeals to a higher authority. As adults we learned that our father believed that he had this obligation, that his function was to represent this higher authority, no matter what, even to the detriment of his family. We came to realize that he did not exercise authority through self-gratification. A higher authority existed, and he was its representative. We could respect our father for accepting the burden.

The authority he represented remained a mystery, but it relied on the idea of impersonal value, working on the assumption that no matter how outlandish an action might appear, it was always for our own good, which did not take us very far. By the end of it I for one had come to recognise that my father exercised authority without being convinced that it was for the best, but if it was for the best then this was by way of a preparation for the injustice we would face throughout our lives, and the survival of the species demanded that we survive it.

After the Merry Blethers

I had been looking for shadows but saw none. That story by Stephen Leacock again, re the naive young minister new to the parish who is visiting the flock on an introductory capacity and arrives in the home of a local family in a rural community who are not 100% glad to see him but nevertheless remain gracious so he has to stay the night because it is too late to travel and next morning for petit dejeuner he cannot say no so he sits and eats—much to the unveiled annoyance of male family members, and again from them at luncheon then later too, following the evening dinner when he is still sitting there suffering the jibes and barbs from other family members, assorted family members, one old lady brandishing a sturdy walking stick—influenced no doubt by Dostoevsky's story about the minor aristocrat who blunders into the wedding party of an employee, steps into the basin of dessert jelly—and eventually, poor lad, in Leacock's story he dies in the house through that same social affliction, the inability to say no through a damnable politeness—unlike Dostoevsky's central character who goes to work the morning after and wonders if it was all a bad dream, but then an elderly clerk appears and smiles, he smiles, and all is alive in this smile; the whole world knows of last night's folly, nothing is as it was and never ever can it return.

Ah but not me not me, no sir, not me! I achieved lift-off from the sagging armchair, and onwards to the exit, waving merrily and saw then a strangely closed door with the loud but guarded rattle of a forbidden sermonic declamation and realized did I that this selfsame door would lead me asunder from annexe to fiery region wherein elemental company assembled round a coefficient of candles glowing dully red, centred in the ghastly dark, and from the shadowy rear appeared the wizened caretaker and goggle-eyed partner, leading a choir in a medley of jolly round-the-campfire folk-psalms of a kind one associates with evangelical organisations developed from the deeds and intellectual preoccupations of certain seventeenth-century mystics.

A small band had shifted to the far side of the moon and were engaged in frantic whispering, armed with their own cargo of booze; elsewhere people chortled and choked from within a set of oratological flipperies led by a rotund fellow of lugubrious countenance. A third band of worthies, smaller in number, were smoking cigarettes by a chimney, quietly, desultorily. I recognised a woman whose name I still could not decipher, and whose eyelids had closed, and whose head nodded on the shoulder of a nervous male fidgeter. In settling an earlier argument I had suggested to this very woman that one of the finest Merlots one had quaffed was purchased in Bordeaux, France; bought in a local Lidl for two Euros. I was convinced of that until discovering there is no Lidl in Bordeaux, France. I said as much to the woman. Yes, replied she, but there may have been an Aldi in the years to which you refer. She was correct. I knew this at once but recognised also that she preferred not to continue our brief dialogue. Why not? I asked, having failed to notice that I had only thought the question but failed to give it voice. All I had had the entire night was water, pure clear water, water. Not one single solitary glass of alcohol. Nevertheless I was stupefied. Fatigue and lack of food. I was starving, and tomorrow the barren wastes.

My presence was superfluous. Time to leave, if only I could find my jaiket which I thought to have left on a chair in the dining room where I had been sitting, laughing at the japes of the host and his family, the last I recalled.

I was snugly encased, the curtains drawn about me, my electronic source tuned to internet radio.

I sighed, seeing that I was not in the dining room after all but in a bedroom of sorts, with piles of coats and jaikets under which the bed and here indeed was I, outstretched, hands clasped behind my head thinking cheerful thoughts of the merry past. Ah, those were the days, I was thinking, one knows not the minute nor the hour but the time is nigh. And when the time is nigh up one gets, shoes on and aff we go. But I was weighed down, weighed down.

About the Author

James Kelman was born in Glasgow, June 1946, and left school in 1961. He travelled about and worked at various jobs. He lives in Glasgow with Marie, who has supported him since 1969.

ABOUT PM PRESS

PM Press is an independent, radical publisher of critically necessary books for our tumultuous times. Our aim is to deliver bold political ideas and vital stories to all walks of life and arm the dreamers to demand the impossible. Founded in 2007 by a small group of people with decades of publishing, media, and organizing experience, we have sold millions of copies of our books, most often one at a time, face to face. We're old enough to know what we're doing and young enough to know what's at stake. Join us to create a better world.

PM Press
PO Box 23912
Oakland, CA 94623
www.pmpress.org

PM Press in Europe
europe@pmpress.org
www.pmpress.org.uk

FRIENDS OF PM PRESS

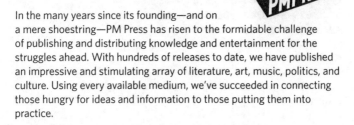

These are indisputably momentous times—the
financial system is melting down globally and
the Empire is stumbling. Now more than ever
there Is a vital need for radical ideas.

In the many years since its founding—and on
a mere shoestring—PM Press has risen to the formidable challenge
of publishing and distributing knowledge and entertainment for the
struggles ahead. With hundreds of releases to date, we have published
an impressive and stimulating array of literature, art, music, politics, and
culture. Using every available medium, we've succeeded in connecting
those hungry for ideas and information to those putting them into
practice.

Friends of PM allows you to directly help impact, amplify, and revitalize
the discourse and actions of radical writers, filmmakers, and artists. It
provides us with a stable foundation from which we can build upon our
early successes and provides a much-needed subsidy for the materials
that can't necessarily pay their own way. You can help make that
happen—and receive every new title automatically delivered to your
door once a month—by joining as a Friend of PM Press. And, we'll throw
in a free T-shirt when you sign up.

Here are your options:

• **$30 a month** Get all books and pamphlets plus a 50% discount on all
  webstore purchases

• **$40 a month** Get all PM Press releases (including CDs and DVDs)
  plus a 50% discount on all webstore purchases

• **$100 a month** Superstar—Everything plus PM merchandise, free
  downloads, and a 50% discount on all webstore purchases

For those who can't afford $30 or more a month, we have **Sustainer
Rates** at $15, $10 and $5. Sustainers get a free PM Press T-shirt and a
50% discount on all purchases from our website.

Your Visa or Mastercard will be billed once a month, until you tell us to
stop. Or until our efforts succeed in bringing the revolution around. Or
the financial meltdown of Capital makes plastic redundant. Whichever
comes first.

All We Have Is the Story: Selected Interviews (1973-2022)

James Kelman

ISBN: 979-8-88744-005-7 (paperback)
      979-8-88744-006-4 (hardcover)
$24.95/$39.95   352 pages

All We Have
Is the Story

Selected Interviews
1973–2022
James Kelman
THE KELMAN LIBRARY

Novelist, playwright, essayist, and master of the short story. Artist and engaged working-class intellectual; husband, father, and grandfather as well as committed revolutionary activist.

From his first publication (a short story collection *An Old Pub Near the Angel* on a tiny American press) through his latest novel (*God's Teeth and Other Phenomena*) and work with Noam Chomsky (*Between Thought and Expression Lies a Lifetime*—both published on a slightly larger American press), *All We Have Is the Story* chronicles the life and work—to date—of "probably the most influential novelist of the post-war period" (*The Times*).

Drawing deeply on a radical tradition that is simultaneously political, philosophical, cultural, and literary, James Kelman articulates the complexities and tensions of the craft of writing; the narrative voice and grammar; imperialism and language; art and value; solidarity and empathy; class and nation-state; and, above all, that it begins and ends with the story.

"One of the things the establishment always does is isolate voices of dissent and make them specific—unique if possible. It's easy to dispense with dissent if you can say there's him in prose and him in poetry. As soon as you say there's him, him, and her there, and that guy here and that woman over there, and there's all these other writers in Africa, and then you've got Ireland, the Caribbean—suddenly there's this kind of mass dissent going on, and that becomes something dangerous, something that the establishment won't want people to relate to and go Christ, you're doing the same as me. Suddenly there's a movement going on. It's fine when it's all these disparate voices; you can contain that. The first thing to do with dissent is say 'You're on your own, you're a phenomenon.' I'm not a phenomenon at all: I'm just a part of what's been happening in prose for a long, long while."
—James Kelman from a 1993 interview

The State Is the Enemy

James Kelman

ISBN: 978-1-62963-968-0 (paperback)
     978-1-62963-976-5 (hardcover)
$19.95/$39.95   256 pages

Incendiary and heartrending, the sixteen essays in *The State Is the Enemy* lay bare government brutality against the working class, immigrants, asylum seekers, ethnic minorities, and all who are deemed of "a lower order." Drawing parallels between atrocities committed against the Kurds by the Turkish State and the racist police brutality and government-sanctioned murders in the UK, James Kelman shatters the myth of Western exceptionalism, revealing the universality of terror campaigns levied against the most vulnerable, and calling on a global citizenry to stand in solidarity with victims of oppression. Kelman's case against the Turkish and British governments is not just a litany of murders, or an impassioned plea—it is a cool-headed takedown of the State and an essential primer for revolutionaries.

"One of the most influential writers of his generation."
  —*The Guardian*

"James Kelman changed my life."
  —Douglas Stuart, author of *Shuggie Bain*

"Probably the most influential novelist of the post-war period."
  —*The Times*

"Kelman has the knack, maybe more than anyone since Joyce, of fixing in his writing the lyricism of ordinary people's speech.... Pure aesthete, undaunted democrat—somehow Kelman manages to reconcile his two halves."
  —*Esquire* (London)

"The greatest British novelist of our time."
  —*Sunday Herald*

"The greatest living British novelist."
  —Amit Chaudhuri, author of *A New World*

"What an enviably, devilishly wonderful writer is James Kelman."
  —John Hawkes, author of *The Blood Oranges*

Keep Moving and No Questions

James Kelman

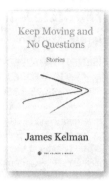

ISBN: 978-1-62963-967-3 (paperback)
978-1-62963-975-8 (hardcover)
$17.95/$29.95   288 pages

James Kelman's inimitable voice brings the stories of lost men to light in these twenty-one tales of down-on-their-luck antiheroes who wander, drink, hatch plans, ponder existence, and survive in an unwelcoming and often comic world. *Keep Moving and No Questions* is a collection of the finest examples of Kelman's facility with dialog, stream-of-consciousness narrative, and sharp cultural observation. Class is always central in these brief glimpses of men abiding the hands they've been dealt. An ideal introduction to Kelman's work and a wonderful edition for fans and Kelman completists, this lovely volume will make clear why James Kelman is known as the greatest living modernist writer.

"*Kelman has the knack, maybe more than anyone since Joyce, of fixing in his writing the lyricism of ordinary people's speech. . . . Pure aesthete, undaunted democrat—somehow Kelman manages to reconcile his two halves.*"
—*Esquire* (London)

God's Teeth and Other Phenomena

James Kelman

ISBN: 978-1-62963-939-0 (paperback)
978-1-62963-940-6 (hardcover)
$17.95/$34.95   368 pages

Jack Proctor, a celebrated older writer and curmudgeon, goes off to residency where he is to be an honored part of teaching and giving public readings but soon finds that the atmosphere of the literary world has changed since his last foray into the public sphere. Unknown to most, unable to work on his own writing, surrounded by a host of odd characters, would-be writers, antagonists, handlers, and members of the elite House of Art and Aesthetics, Proctor finds himself driven to distraction (literally in a very tiny car). This is a story of a man attempting not to go mad when forced to stop his own writing in order to coach others to write. Proctor's tour of rural places, pubs, theaters, and fancy parties, where he is to be headlining as a "Banker Prize winner," reads like a literary version of *This Is Spinal Tap*. Uproariously funny, brilliantly philosophical, gorgeously written, this is James Kelman at his best.

James Kelman was born in Glasgow, June 1946, and left school in 1961. He began work in the printing trade then moved around, working in various jobs in various places. He was living in England when he started writing: ramblings, musings, sundry phantasmagoria. He committed to it and kept at it. In 1969 he met and married Marie Connors from South Wales. They settled in Glasgow and still live there, not far from their kids and grandkids. He still plugs away at the ramblings, musings, politicking and so on, supported by the same lady.

"God's Teeth and Other Phenomena *is electric. Forget all the rubbish you've been told about how to write, the requirements of the marketplace and the much vaunted 'readability' that is supposed to be sacrosanct. This is a book about how art gets made, its murky, obsessive, unedifying demands and the endless, sometimes hilarious, humiliations literary life inflicts on even its most successful names."*
—Eimear McBride, author of *A Girl is a Half-Formed Thing* and *The Lesser Bohemians*

Between Thought and Expression Lies a Lifetime: Why Ideas Matter

Noam Chomsky & James Kelman

ISBN: 978-1-62963-880-5 (paperback)
978-1-62963-886-7 (hardcover)
$19.95/$39.95   304 pages

"The world is full of information. What do we do when we get the information, when we have digested the information, what do we do then? Is there a point where ye say, yes, stop, now I shall move on."

This exhilarating collection of essays, interviews, and correspondence—spanning the years 1988 through 2018, and reaching back a decade more—is about the simple concept that ideas matter. They mutate, inform, create fuel for thought, and inspire actions.

As Kelman says, the State relies on our suffocation, that we cannot hope to learn "the truth. But whether we can or not is beside the point. We must grasp the nettle, we assume control and go forward."

Between Thought and Expression Lies a Lifetime is an impassioned, elucidating, and often humorous collaboration. Philosophical and intimate, it is a call to ponder, imagine, explore, and act.

"The real reason Kelman, despite his stature and reputation, remains something of a literary outsider is not, I suspect, so much that great, radical Modernist writers aren't supposed to come from working-class Glasgow, as that great, radical Modernist writers are supposed to be dead. Dead, and wrapped up in a Penguin Classic: that's when it's safe to regret that their work was underappreciated or misunderstood (or how little they were paid) in their lifetimes. You can write what you like about Beckett or Kafka and know they're not going to come round and tell you you're talking nonsense, or confound your expectations with a new work. Kelman is still alive, still writing great books, climbing."
—James Meek, *London Review of Books*

"A true original. . . . A real artist. . . . It's now very difficult to see which of [Kelman's] peers can seriously be ranked alongside him without ironic eyebrows being raised."
—Irvine Welsh, *The Guardian*

RUIN

Cara Hoffman

ISBN: 978-1-62963-929-1 (paperback)
**   978-1-62963-931-4 (hardcover)**
$14.95/$25.95   128 pages

A little girl who disguises herself as an old man, an addict who collects dollhouse furniture, a crime reporter confronted by a talking dog, a painter trying to prove the non-existence of god, and lovers in a penal colony who communicate through technical drawings—these are just a few of the characters who live among the ruins. Cara Hoffman's short fictions are brutal, surreal, hilarious, and transgressive, celebrating the sharp beauty of outsiders and the infinitely creative ways humans muster psychic resistance under oppressive conditions. *RUIN* is both bracingly timely and eerily timeless in its examination of an American state in free-fall: unsparing in its disregard for broken, ineffectual institutions, while shining with compassion for the damaged left in their wake. The ultimate effect of these ten interconnected stories is one of invigoration and a sense of possibilities—hope for a new world extracted from the rubble of the old.

Cara Hoffman is the author of three New York Times Editors' Choice novels; the most recent, *Running*, was named a Best Book of the Year by *Esquire* magazine. She first received national attention in 2011 with the publication of *So Much Pretty* which sparked a national dialogue on violence and retribution, and was named a Best Novel of the Year by *The New York Times Book Review*. Her second novel, *Be Safe I Love You*, was nominated for a Folio Prize, named one of the Five Best Modern War Novels, and awarded a Sundance Global Filmmaking Award. A MacDowell Fellow and an Edward Albee Fellow, she has lectured at Oxford University's Rhodes Global Scholars Symposium and at the Renewing the Anarchist Tradition Conference. Her work has appeared in *The New York Times*, *Paris Review*, *BOMB*, *Bookforum*, *Rolling Stone*, *Daily Beast*, and on NPR. A founding editor of *The Anarchist Review of Books*, and part of the Athens Workshop collective, she lives in Athens, Greece, with her partner.

"*RUIN is a collection of ten jewels, each multi-faceted and glittering, to be experienced with awe and joy. Cara Hoffman has seen a secret world right next to our own, just around the corner, and written us a field guide to what she's found. I love this book.*"
—Sara Gran, author of *Infinite Blacktop* and *Claire Dewitt and the City of the Dead*

The Colonel Pyat Quartet

Michael Moorcock
with introductions by Alan Wall

Byzantium Endures
ISBN: 978-1-60486-491-5
$22.00   400 pages

The Laughter of Carthage
ISBN: 978-1-60486-492-2
$22.00   448 pages

Jerusalem Commands
ISBN: 978-1-60486-493-9
$22.00   448 pages

The Vengeance of Rome
ISBN: 978-1-60486-494-6
$23.00   500 pages

Moorcock's Pyat Quartet has been described as an authentic masterpiece of the 20th and 21st centuries. It's the story of Maxim Arturovitch Pyatnitski, a cocaine addict, sexual adventurer, and obsessive anti-Semite whose epic journey from Leningrad to London connects him with scoundrels and heroes from Trotsky to Makhno, and whose career echoes that of the 20th century's descent into Fascism and total war.

It is Michael Moorcock's extraordinary achievement to convert the life of Maxim Pyatnitski into epic and often hilariously comic adventure. Sustained by his dreams and profligate inventions, his determination to turn his back on the realities of his own origins, Pyat runs from crisis to crisis, every ruse a further link in a vast chain of deceit, suppression, betrayal. Yet, in his deranged self-deception, his monumentally distorted vision, this thoroughly unreliable narrator becomes a lens for focusing, through the dimensions of wild farce and chilling terror, on an uneasy brand of truth.

We, the Children of Cats

Tomoyuki Hoshino
Translated by Brian Bergstrom

ISBN: 978-1-60486-591-2
$20.00   288 pages

A man and woman find their genders and
sexualities brought radically into question when
their bodies sprout new parts, seemingly out of
thin air. . . . A man travels from Japan to Latin
America in search of revolutionary purpose
and finds much more than he bargains for. . . . A journalist investigates
a poisoning at an elementary school and gets lost in an underworld
of buried crimes, secret societies, and haunted forests. . . . Two young
killers, exiled from Japan, find a new beginning as resistance fighters in
Peru. . . .

These are but a few of the stories told in *We, the Children of Cats*, a new
collection of provocative early works by Tomoyuki Hoshino, winner
of the 2011 Kenzaburo Oe Award in Literature and author of the
powerhouse novel *Lonely Hearts Killer* (PM Press, 2009). Drawing on
sources as diverse as Borges, Nabokov, García Márquez, Kenji Nakagami
and traditional Japanese folklore, Hoshino creates a challenging, slyly
subversive literary world all his own. By turns teasing and terrifying,
laconic and luminous, the stories in this anthology demonstrate
Hoshino's view of literature as "an art that wavers, like a heat shimmer,
between joy at the prospect of becoming something else and despair at
knowing that such a transformation is ultimately impossible . . . a novel's
words trace the pattern of scars left by the struggle between these two
feelings." Blending an uncompromising ethical vision with exuberant,
freewheeling imagery and bracing formal experimentation, the five
short stories and three novellas included in *We, the Children of Cats* show
the full range and force of Hoshino's imagination; the anthology also
includes an afterword by translator and editor Brian Bergstrom and a
new preface by Hoshino himself.

"These wonderful stories make you laugh and cry, but mostly they astonish,
co-mingling daily reality with the envelope pushed to the max and the
interstice of the hard edges of life with the profoundly gentle ones."
—Helen Mitsios, editor of *New Japanese Voices: The Best Contemporary*
Fiction from Japan and *Digital Geishas and Talking Frogs: The Best 21st*
Century Short Stories from Japan

The Collapsing Frontier

Jonathan Lethem

ISBN: 978-1-62963-488-3
      979-8-88744-029-3
$16.00/$24.95   176 pages

This collection compiles his intensely
personal thoughts on the most interesting
and deplorable topics in post-postmodern
America. It moves from original new fiction to
insights on popular culture, cult and canonical
authors, and problematic people.

Plus...

"David Bowman and the Furry-Girl School of American Fiction" is a
personal true adventure, as Lethem tries (with the help of a seeming
expert) to elbow his way into literary respectability. "The Collapsing
Frontier" and "In Mugwump Four" are fictions mapping ominous new
realms. "Calvino's 'Lightness' and the Feral Child of History" is an
intimate encounter with a legendary author. In "My Year of Reading
Lemmishly" and "Snowden in the Labyrinth" he explores courage, art,
and the search for truth, with wildly different results.

And Featuring: Our usual Outspoken Interview, in which Lethem reveals
the secret subtext of his books, how he spent his MacArthur award
money, and how a Toyota he owned was used in the robbery of a fast-
food restaurant.

*"Lethem is one of our most perceptive cultural critics, conversant in both the
high and low realms, his insights buffeted by his descriptive imagination."*
—Los Angeles Times Book Review

"One of America's greatest storytellers."
—The Washington Post

"Lethem has talent to burn."
—Village Voice Literary Supplement

*"Aside from being one of the most inventive writers on the planet, Lethem is
also one of the funniest."*
—San Francisco Examiner